After Midnight

Nelle Kessler

Contents

CHAPTER 1

N OVA

One word.

Fucker.

I had more in the inventory but I stared at Paul from across the table with nothing but a hateful glare. I hated him. I hated that place. My lips curled into disgust as I witnessed his condescending smirk widen with amusement.

I was pissed. I was upset. I was in the right mind to get into my car and wedge my boss between a wall and my bumper. Ex-boss.

Maybe I'd reverse a couple of times too.

"A Friday morning?" I asked, my voice thick and laced with annoyance.

I should have taken a computer home with me for the inconvenience of being fired before I started my shift. He couldn't have waited? He couldn't have done it the previous day?

Fuck you, I wanted to say. I wanted to cuss out loud and release months of pent up frustration. I didn't. Despite raging, Paul was my reference for other jobs. Without a good word from him, I'd never find a job in a pitiful and dreary bank ever again.

What was my life?

"I wanted to see your pretty face one last time," he muttered, chuckling as he sat down on his rustic computer chair as if it were his throne.

I always hated his laugh. It was the worst kind. The type of laugh that said 'I'm a boss and I cannot be fucked with. I do the fucking'

From across the room, I thought about how I'd never have to spend another day with the stench of his expensive cologne wafting across the small office. It was unbearable. It almost always gave me a headache.

I did a slight roll of my eyes and turned on my heel, heading to my little cubical to collect my succulents and other nick-nicks I refused to leave in the hands of the other vultures in the office.

No more stealing of my lunch.

No more unplugging my computer just to piss me off.

No more of anything.

Relieved? Yes. Hopelessly stressed about my sudden lack of paycheque every two weeks? Yes.

"Novs," he called out the awful nickname he had for me. "Don't forget."

I turned back to him, finding his elbow propped up onto his table while he waved a flimsy piece of paper around. I eyed him, wondering if the asshole was going to make me walk up to him for the money he owed me.

He nodded his head, gesturing for me to approach him and it confirmed that he was indeed as slimy as I thought he was. Taking a deep breath in, I swallowed away all sense of pride just to walk back to his desk and hold my hand out.

"Nuh-uh," he tsked, shaking his greying head. "Come around and take it from my hand, Nova."

"Really, Paul?" I asked, giving him a bored look.

Did he have a humiliation kink? Is that what it was?

"I mean," he started, lifting one shoulder in a shrug. "If you want it, I think it's only fair you get it yourself. Right?"

"Set it on the table then," I said the first thing that came to mind. I didn't want to go over there. I didn't want to be close to him. Paul never touched me, but he always hovered a little too close for comfort—almost as if saying if I want to, I can.

"How rude of you," he muttered, pursing his lips in disapproval while he shook his head.

I had all the time in the world to stand there and stare at him, but my hand itched to slap the silly smirk off his face. Surely his face had to be tired by now. I bit down on my molars, feeling my chest grow tight with anger as I let my feet take me over to his side of the desk.

His eyes followed me as if I were his own personal lap dancer. It gave me chills. A shiver of disgust raced through me, but I reached out to snatch the paper with a restraint that I didn't know I possessed. He pulled back just in time.

What the hell was wrong with him?

How could I fight for the money he owed me?

"Nova," he drawled, leaning back on his chair. "Say pleas-"

"Fuck off, Paul," I muttered, quickening my speed and grabbing the paper before the both of us could blink.

He was visibly shocked, and highly amused. Sick fuck. Perhaps I was better off not working there. I turned around to leave before he could say a word, listening to his brazen chuckle follow me out the door.

"Maybe loosen a button or two, Novs! You'll have an easier time finding a job," he blurted, loud enough for the office to hear.

It wasn't surprising he said stupid shit like that. I didn't bother with a reply, needing to retreat to my car before I ended up with a criminal record. First, I needed to stop at my cubicle.

"You know he can't do that, right?" a voice asked behind me. It was Spencer—a frat boy turned banker. He was charming, but he did try to fuck me one night when we went out for drinks. It was hard to look at him the same after that considering we worked together.

Not anymore. Maybe he'd be a stress reliever.

No, Spencer wasn't my type. He was nice to look at, but there was something boy next door about him that I had no interest in. A little too...safe.

"Do what?" I asked, grabbing all of my things and stuffing it into my handbag. I paused, staring at the outdated computer and realising I couldn't even take one of those for a quick buck. It seemed cheap, and on the brink of falling apart. I almost kicked my desk.

"Fire you without warning," he said, his voice decorated with a slight accent.

"I know," I said, still annoyed that I was in a pencil skirt and heels when I could have slept in.

"Then why are you just taking it, Nova?" he asked, and I turned to find a frown on his brows. Spencer was just a little taller than me, a bit on the lean side and dressed in his usual attire—brown slacks and a polo shirt. He was also a dirty blonde who had no desire to get a haircut.

"Because I'm not in the mood to fight," I said, breathing out exasperatedly. The place wasn't worth fighting for.

"So you're just going to be jobless?" Spencer asked, and I was surprised he wasn't making a joke of it like he did with everything else. His face was serious and I stilled, looking at him. I needed to get out of there before I was blinded by rage.

"Would you fight to stay here?" I asked him, placing my last succulent into my bag without taking my eyes off him.

"No, but—"

"Exactly. You know I wanted to leave here six months ago," I explained, sighing. "Now I have a reason to." The reason being that Paul promoted the assistant he had been fucking to my job. I wasn't mad at her—but I was deeply disgusted that Paul had no line.

"Nova."

"Spencer.

"Who am I going to have coffee with?"

I gazed at him, feeling slightly defeated. Spencer was a friend I wasn't going to see anymore, and there was a high chance we were never going to speak again. Did I care much for it? Honestly, I'd probably never think about him again.

"You have my number," I added, just because.

He grinned—that same charming grin that lit the office up and I shook my head at the sneaky little bastard. Quickly, he didn't seem sad anymore. Instead, everything about him had suddenly morphed into nothing but flirtatious and then I remembered who he was. My hands stilled on the objects I had been picking up, eyeing Spencer with a look of boredom.

"So I can call you?" he asked, smiling as he leaned his arm against the cabinet. "And ask you on a date? Since we're no longer co-workers?"

"No, Spencer," I deadpanned, rolling my eyes.

"You just said—"

"I know what I said," I blurted. What was wrong with everyone in this office? "I'm leaving now, Spencer. Call me for coffee. Nothing else."

"But—"

I raised my hand, silently stopping him and his parted lips closed. With a silent wave from me, I made my way through the security gates with the thought that I'd never step foot in that place again.

Wait. I stopped in my tracks when I remembered my coffee flask still sat in the kitchen. Knowing my colleagues, one of them will take it for themselves.

I continued my walk to my car, listening to the rustling of morning traffic and construction happening in the distance. It was early, and I rushed home with the intention of sleeping the day away. My apartment was at least a thirty minute drive from the bank—fifteen minutes if I used the highway and I went with the latter.

It was only nine when I reached home. As soon as I stepped into my place—I undressed myself, loosened the bun on my head and washed my make-up off.

It took me five minutes to get into bed and even less to fall asleep.

When my slumber finally left me, I woke up in complete darkness and as confused as ever. Oh, right, I was fired. Or retrenched as Paul would say.

Groggy, I wiped my eyes and cuddled into my duvet with a sigh that was nothing short of blissful. It felt good to sleep without disturbances. It felt even better sleeping without the dreadful thought of having to plaster a fake customer service smile and raise my voice an octave higher.

At that point, I was just trying to make myself better about being unemployed.

My hand reached out from under my covers, blindly finding my phone until the screen lit up and showed I had slept for a total of eleven hours.

"Shit," I mumbled. Was I that sleep deprived? Considering that I worked six days and three nights a week, it wasn't surprising I woke up when I was supposed to be getting ready for bed.

Fuck it.

I needed to get my shit together

With a new found will for life, I slid the covers off me and sat up. Breathing in, I thought about meeting up with my friend Jade. Friday night? She must have been working but I called anyway and I was right. Jade was a nurse—a redhead with a bold personality who did piercings on the side.

I looked up at my ceiling, pondering on my options but it wasn't as if I had many. Spencer? No, he'd think I'm calling to hook up. Ethan, my brother? No, he always acted like a fucking dad.

My cousin, Riley? She was a newlywed who had a recently birthed a baby boy. I groaned, half annoyed that I lacked friends and fully annoyed that I felt as if I couldn't go out alone.

Wait. Who said I couldn't?

Solo for the night didn't seem like a bad idea.

There was nothing wrong with it, right? I was in the mood for a drink and music with a few pretty faces to look at. When was the last time I went out? Or wore anything besides an outdated work skirt and a blouse?

I glanced over at my closed closet, hoping that the black number I wore a while ago still fit me.

Forgetting the dress, I headed over to my shower and discarded of my clothes along the way. I have to pick that up later.

In one day, I managed to feel better than I did in weeks—in months.

And I knew the second I stepped underneath the hot stream of water that I had no intention of spending the night sulking at home.

CHAPTER 2

I curled my hand around the thick glass holding my liquor of the night—silently regretting my choice as I sat at the bar. White rum. What the fuck was I thinking? It was unusual choice that ran expensive.

However, that wasn't my main concern.

A man was dangerously close to me, hovering almost as I felt his body temperature on my bare arm.

From the corner of my eye, I could tell he was tall and brunette. A combination I would have taken home with me on any other day. Tonight, I wasn't looking for a quick fuck. I wanted a quick drink and a long night of enjoying the music.

"Can I help you?" I asked, averting my gaze to the brunette nearly leaning over me.

I stopped myself from rolling my eyes at the sloppiness in his body language. He had a lazy smile on his face as he learned his elbow on the countertop, watching me with a grin that didn't reach his eyes. I let out a sigh, finding the lust written all over his face too unflattering to look at.

"Nah. Can I help you, though? You seem a little tense," he whispered, barely audible over the live band playing in the background.

I inched away from the alcohol fumes on his breath but it wasn't his overly confidence that caught my attention. Or the cartoon print on his t-shirt. No, it was the silver band wrapped around his ring finger. The asshole even lacked the decency to take it off.

My brows pinched together into an unstoppable frown. If it wasn't an old fuck hitting on me, it was a man with a wife and kids at home and both made me feel equally disgusted. I didn't say anything but I closed my palm over my glass when I looked away from it.

"No?" he asked, chuckling as if I were his entertainment.

"You're married," I breathed, irritated.

"That's a problem?" he asked, stroking his ring with the pad of his thumb. I was too taken aback by his shamelessness to say anything else.

I should take my ass home.

"Okay," he murmured, shrugging. "I can take it off if you want."

I scoffed, finishing off the last of my rum.

"Please," I emphasised, giving him a look that must have translated into pure disgust. "Just go away." He wasn't my type anyway.

"Look—I pay well," he said, hurriedly pulling out his wallet. "Whatever your rate is, I'll double it."

My jaw dropped, but it was still hard to be surprised. In a way, my brain found it as a stupid compliment and I looked down at my pretty little dress. Yes, it still fits.

"Oh, you're not..." he trailed off, his own face turning bright red. "Fuck. I'm sorry. You're just—you were sitting all alone so I assumed you were selling—I mean."

"Go."

"Yes, I'll fuck off now."

The man rushed off and I let out the eye roll I'd been holding back on. Honestly, it wasn't the first time I'd been mistaken for an escort. I was sitting alone—all dolled up as I eyed the place. Could I blame him? No. Could I wish his wife left him broke and lonely? Yes.

I let out a sigh, realising the night was not turning out how I thought it would.

Maybe I should have put an end to my attempt at enjoying myself right then.

But I didn't.

Regretfully, the casino I sat in wasn't my first choice. It wasn't my second either. Every other place was packed to the brim. If it wasn't outrageously full, it was unbelievably empty—dead. The casino was small and mostly bar, but it was the only place I managed to find on the strip that didn't feel life threatening.

I gazed around one more time, finding the place mostly decorated with women in sparkly cocktail dresses and men in black tuxedos.

The smell of tobacco lingered in the air, and I remembered the chain-smoker my mother was. She eventually quit—not willingly and knowingly, though. She passed away with a cigarette in her fucking hand.

I nearly chuckled out loud but that would have made me seem crazy, right?

Wanting a second drink, I decided to stay a few more minutes. I didn't want to get absolutely plastered, but I was craving a slight buzz while I thought about flattening Paul underneath my car and visiting my mother's grave afterwards.

What am I meant to do with myself now?

"Another for you, miss?" the bartender asked, his eyes covered by reading glasses.

Miss?

He leaned both hands on the counter, a friendly smile on his face. He kind of resembled Ethan and I almost scowled. When was the last time my brother texted me? Or called? Or acknowledged my existence?

When was the last time I did those things too?

"Uhm, no. Can you make it a daiquiri, please?" I murmured, finally taking my purse off my shoulder and then setting it on the bar.

I needed to relax.

The bartender nodded, grabbing the towel from his shoulder and heading to the far end of the bar. I watched him make my drink, shifting in my seat to get comfortable but it was soon proven entirely too hard to do so on an uncomfortable stool.

My ass was starting to ache.

The bartender finally settled my drink in front of me, and I thanked him with a small smile while my hand wrapped around the cocktail glass.

I took a sip, sighing at the taste of something other than the bitterness of pure rum. Vinny the bartender did a good job in less than thirty seconds. Finally feeling at peace, I observed my surroundings and noticed three things.

One; the man that had been bothering me a few minutes ago had found his new victim. A beautiful blonde girl was visibly uncomfortable—fake laughing at his jokes until her friend came to her rescue. The man's shoulders dropped as he watched the two woman walk away from him. I chuckled. What a loser.

Two; a man had walked into the casino.

Three; he was a really gorgeous man who walked as if he was there for a purpose. I looked away. I could look at pretty people but I couldn't find it in me to look at attractive people.

Did that make sense? In my head, it did.

I focused on my drink and there wasn't much to look at except a working Vinny and the array of expensive drinks behind him. I did the one thing I always did when I wanted to pretend I was busy—I pulled out my phone and read the unexpected text from Spencer.

Immediately feeling a damper on my mood, my eyes skimmed the words and realised he was asking me out for a coffee.

How many times have I rolled my eyes tonight?

But seeing Spencer's name reminded me of that stupid place. I didn't reply, but instead I pulled out the cheque Paul had given me.

All I wanted to do was look at it. I had no savings. I had no pocket money. All I had was that cheque. I grabbed it, holding it with both hands and staring at it as if it were my lifeline. In a way, it was. It was rent. It was juice for my car.

Looking at the amount, I felt my face fall.

Instead of a paycheque worth three months of work as he had promised. I was only given a month and a half.

I sighed, dropping my head into the palm of my hand. All I need-ed was a half done cigarette between my fingertips to embody the most stressed out person alive.

What the fuck am I meant to do now? I needed to start looking for a new job yesterday.

Why was I sitting in the casino when I could have been on my laptop searching for a way to make money?

I looked at the married man still trying his luck, considering my options. He did say he'd double whatever my rate was. I cracked a small smile, shaking my head as I thought about how utterly fucked I was.

"That's crazy," I muttered, sighing as my eyes watched the drink I was about to pay twenty bucks for.

"What is?"

I stopped mid-sip and turned to look next to me, finding the man who had walked in two minutes ago now ordering a drink of his own. Oh. He's tall, and brunette.

"Nothing," I answered, meaning it. Was it really any of his business? I looked at him again, trying to act as if I were completely unfazed by the striking features on his face.

What accent is that? He nodded, and a drink from Vinny was slid his way. I don't remember hearing him say anything—let alone order an entire drink next to me.

"It's good to see you, Ramiro. Damn. How long has it been?" Vinny asked, his grin wide and cheery.

Ramiro.

I didn't want to intrude on the conversation, and it genuinely felt as if I was. I breathed in, rolling my neck while Ramiro told Vinny it had been two months. Was Ramiro hot or was I desperate for a way to decompress?

I gazed at him quickly. No, he was definitely hot. Not married man hot—or Spencer hot. The type of hot that meant he probably didn't fuck good. It was always the most stunning men who had a hard time focusing on anybody but themselves.

I need to stop.

I snapped out of my thoughts, finding Vinny talking to a different customer and not Ramiro.

But he was still next to me.

"Listen," he murmured, catching my attention. "It's none of my business, I know. But you need to put that away before someone takes it from you."

"What?" I asked dumbly, the glass in my hand stopping mid-air. Oh, right. The cheque. I grabbed it, placing it neatly into my purse. How embarrassing. He saw my payslip.

He smiled and underneath the dimming light of the bar, the little dents on his cheeks were the first thing I noticed. Dimples. Okay, I really needed to leave.

How fucking bias was I?

"Thank you," I murmured, finally looking at him long enough to notice the tattoos creeping out of the collar of his shirt.

Let's leave.

I gazed down in search for a ring, but there were none on his ring finger and one on his index—complimented by more ink on the back of his hand.

Nah, I need to go.

I grabbed my purse, giving Vinny a small gesture indicating I was ready to pay and fuck off. Ramiro seemed like the type of person I'd take home. Or have him take me home. The way he looked at me, it seemed like he wouldn't mind either option.

"Where are you rushing off to?" he asked, frowning down at me but I could tell the answer probably didn't mean much to him.

Away from you because I was prejudiced and weak against my own resolve.

"It's late, is it not?" I asked, scowling back at him.

"Eleven is late for you?" he asked, looking down at his watch.

Could I drive? Was I over the limit? I probably was even though I suddenly felt beyond sober.

"It is, actually," I answered, the corner of my lips tilting into a small smile. Work would usually have me crashing out by nine, but I slept so long that day that I still felt wide awake.

Instead of asking for the bill, I asked Vinny for a bottle of water instead.

"I never got your name," Vinny murmured, sliding the clear bottle of water my way. "You just—you've been sitting here a while, it'd be nice to know your name."

Wow. I almost threw the bottle against his forehead for indirectly calling me a loser. Hearing Ramiro's discreet laugh was the icing on the cake.

Swallowing everything else I wanted to say, I blurted out with a tight smile, "Nova."

We shook hands like normal, civilised people did and I watched him tend to the next customer afterwards.

"A while, huh?" Ramiro asked with a slight chuckle, his voice deep and accented. It wasn't hard to hear him, but I suddenly wished the music wasn't as loud as it was.

I wanted to hear him properly.

His eyes were glinting with amusement but underneath all of that, there was something I couldn't quite put my finger on.

"Yeah," I muttered, turning on my stool. I faced him, but his gaze didn't waver. Did I want it to? I didn't know yet. He stared at me in the eye and didn't glance lower.

I did.

I looked at the collar of his shirt and found interest in the little silver peeking through. Did I want to trace lower? Absolutely. But I didn't. What was wrong with me? He had spoken a total of five sentences to me and I was starting to retract my previous thought about stunning men.

"Are you waiting for someone?" he asked, a little curiosity in his tone.

What is your motive, Ramiro?

"Are you?" I asked, almost rhetorical but I ached to know the answer and he didn't hesitate to give me one.

"No, I'm not," he said, his eyes locked on mine as if he'd known me for years. "But I don't know. It feels like I'm waiting now."

A small smile spread across my lips. There was a certain intensity about Ramiro. He was hard to read and yet he came off as an open book. He didn't walk in alone. He walked in with three other men who scouted the place as if they were looking for someone.

I thought about my way forward. One night with a man I'd never see again? Or do I head home and guarantee a peaceful sleep?

"Yeah?" I murmured, a small scowl on my brows. "What are you really here for, Ramiro?"

He chuckled, looking away. "I didn't introduce myself to you, Nova."

We're both eavesdroppers.

"I know," I muttered, shrugging. "You're kind of rude."

"I am," he admitted, nodding his head and I couldn't help but crack a small smile at his boldness. "I'm sorry."

I let out a short breath. "No, I'm not waiting for anybody."

Well, I might be now.

"Good," he said, his eyes serious but playful—an odd combination while the corners of his lips pulled up into a smirk. I thought about him while I looked at him.

When was the last time I fucked someone I had just met? Did I ever do that? The answer was a hard no. I always waited. I liked the way he looked at me and I thought about how there was always a first time for everything.

Right?

I felt my heart race, watching as his intense gaze forgot about staying on my face. He looked everywhere. I had my hair down and it nearly covered my cleavage, but he travelled lower and lower until he reached my bare legs.

I almost moved in my seat, but he would have known that I enjoyed the way he analysed me as if I were a favourite painting of his.

If any other man looks at me like that I'd scream my head off. But Ramiro looked good and he smelled good too.

There was nothing arrogant floating off him and it was the one thing I couldn't stand when guys approached me. He seemed like he'd leave me alone if I told him to.

Why am I speaking as if I know this man?

"You didn't answer my question." I finally found my voice.

"What was it, Nova?" he asked, his eyes snapping to mine as if my words were all he wanted to hear.

I scoffed a small chuckle. "It doesn't matter."

I already knew.

He breathed in deeply, letting out a small sigh when he leaned his elbows on the bar. When he made eye-contact, I saw the question he didn't say out loud.

I wanted him to. I had no intention of leaving with anyone when I got there, but Ramiro had quickly changed the trajectory. I didn't even fucking care.

"What do you say, Nova?" he asked, his voice soft and dangerously low.

I was scared to answer—scared of how easy it was for him to change my mind. I wanted it. I wanted it the longer I stared at him and the effect it had on him. He didn't hide it. He showed that he liked what he was looking at. I swallowed away the nerves I tried to conceal, but he could probably see right through me.

"Yes."

Ramiro was quick to get off his chair, downing the last of his drink.

Fuck.

When he reached his hand out to me, I took it and he helped me off my own stool. Fuck. Put on your fucking big girl pants, Nova.

Just do it.

His hand was big—tattooed and the coldness of his ring felt right on my skin. My heart pounded in my chest, but I couldn't deny the unbelievable excitement racing through me.

The both of us were standing and I lifted my head, his height part of the reason I couldn't decide if I wanted to end up at his place or mine. The bar had darkened significantly, signalling the approach of midnight and I took advantage of the lack of light.

It'd be crazy for anyone to see us.

I tugged at his hand and he caught the hint, a small smirk on his lips before he leaned down. The both of us were impatient, but I needed to know if I was acting out on a whim or if I really just wanted to fuck him.

There was only one way to find out.

He kissed me, hard and soft and everything else I expected it to be. His lips were gentle, and he tasted of the drink he just had. Tequila. The inside of my thighs throbbed and I pushed him away, grabbing my purse and a few notes.

Yes, I wanted to. No, maybe I needed to.

He looked visibly dazed and I watched him want more. He reached out for me again but I took his hand instead.

"Where are we going, Ramiro?"

He smiled lazily, swiping his lower lip with the pad of his thumb. "Anywhere you want to be."

"Yours then," I muttered, feeling Ramiro pull at my hand without any rebuttal.

When he started leading us out with a certain eagerness, I couldn't help but think of the last time I felt that way—that nervous, that scared and most of all, that fucking excited.

I hid my smile on the way out.

Maybe I was wrong about not wanting a quick fuck.

CHAPTER 3

I wanted it, I knew that. But what if Ramiro just decides to kill me?

What if turning back was no longer an option?

What if I told myself to stop thinking and enjoy the moment?

He held my hand, pulling me through the front door of his home and I let him.

I was alone with him. I was at his disposal. I was literally his to use and it was a situation I never thought I'd find myself in. I willed away all my doubts, unable to wait for him anymore.

Ramiro closed the door behind him, locking it. Fuck.

What did he do for a living? His place was nice. A little too nice. His loft was on a high building, overlooking the city and I wondered if those cars he parked next to were his own. Did it matter? No, it was better not knowing.

"Ramiro," I murmured, watching as he approached me.

Shit, he looked good. In his white shirt, the muscles on his arms flexed underneath the material. I wanted to feel him and see him and I almost reached out to him. I didn't.

"Nova," he whispered, his dark eyes fixated on mine.

Did he know how good he made my name sound? Was he aware of the effect he had on me? He lifted a tattooed hand and hooked two fingers underneath the strap of my dress, smiling when my breath shuddered.

Why am I so fucking easy?

"Nervous?" he asked, his voice low.

Yes.

I didn't say anything. He must have known that I was. I watched as he leaned lower, maintaining an eye contact that had my body pulsing with heat.

Ramiro was intimidating in an amazing and terrifying way and I couldn't get enough of it. Am I insane? His body was strong—obviously athletic. He worked hard and it showed. He could probably snap me in two if he wanted.

"You shouldn't be," he breathed out, laying a soft kiss on the side of my neck. "You're in control."

"Yeah?" I whispered out, barely capable of focusing on his words when his soft lips touched my jaw.

"Of course," he whispered. "You want me to fuck you? Say the word. You want me to drive you home? Say the word."

Shit. The latter option seemed like the worst one. I didn't want that. I closed my arms around his neck, feeling his smirk on my skin when he realised which one I chose.

I'm already so wet.

He could probably feel my pulse.

Ramiro pulled back and I nearly whined out a protest. Don't stop touching me. He towered over me, dauntingly so and I craned my neck to look up at him. Still feeling the ghostly sensation of his lips on my skin, I wanted more. I probably needed more.

"Can you kiss me, Nova?" he said gently, his fingertips tracing over the length of my arm.

I didn't hesitate. Pushing all self-restraint to the side, I pulled him lower and kissed him hard. My lips touched his and he gasped into my mouth, showing that he wasn't expecting the force behind it. I was tired of fucking around and I'm sure he was too.

He held back, I could tell. He didn't want to scare me off but I was far past that point.

"Oh, fuck," he whispered, his dick pressing into my stomach. He's hard.

I held him tighter and he moaned, curling his arms around my waist and finding my ass in his palms. It sent me into a frenzy.

His hands were big and he squeezed me, lighting a fire within me that felt unfamiliar and foreign.

I groaned, feeling his bulge pressed firmly against me. He's big. It reminded me that it had been a year since I was with anyone. Or was it two years? I couldn't remember. His tongue touched mine and I moaned at the taste of him. Fuck, I'm throbbing.

He groaned, slipping underneath my loose dress and he cupped my bare skin. I was lifted off my heels and my legs closed around his waist, feeling him walk until I was set on a hard table. He carried me with ease and not once did he break away from our kiss.

Our impatient, rough and deep kiss.

I leaned back on my palms, spreading my legs and hoping he'd come closer. He did. I felt him. I felt how hard he was. I felt how badly he wanted it. The wooden table was cold against my skin, but Ramiro was warm and I relished in it.

He pushed into me and I widened my legs, gasping when the front of him pressed against my underwear.

I thought about all the ways I'd let him have me on that very table.

He bit my lip and I felt him shift, sighing as he blindly did whatever he was doing. With no vision, my senses were heightened and I wondered if he was getting a condom. He dragged a drawer open and placed an object inside of it, quickly shutting it.

I stopped moving and opened my eyes, pushing at his shoulders to get a look at him.

"Ramiro," I murmured, still slightly out of breath.

"Yeah?" he whispered, his eyes half-lidded and dazed.

Was he drunk on our kiss?

"What was that?" I asked, slowly dragging my nails over the front of his shirt.

His chest was hard, and I flicked a button open because I couldn't resist. His silver chain peeked through, and I traced the links with my fingertips. Expensive.

Ramiro's smile widened and he slowly leaned closer.

With soft eyes and a low voice, he asked, "What was what?"

I gave him a look. Really? I glanced down at the drawer and opened it, still seeing Ramiro looking at me from my peripheral.

Did he have that on him the entire time? What the fuck did Ramiro do for a living? I gazed back at him, finding an interesting expression on his face. Curiosity. He waited to see how I'd react. I didn't know how to, but I had one question.

How did the casino allow Ramiro inside with a gun?

"Were you planning on killing me, Ramiro?" I murmured, sliding my finger along his belt. He chuckled at my question and I couldn't help but smile at him. His laugh was cute—in a deep and baritone way.

This man could kill me right now if he wanted to.

"No," he murmured, slipping underneath my dress to caress my thighs. "Why would I do that?"

"Where was it?" I asked, letting the tips of my fingers graze over his zipper.

How could I have missed it? It must have been tucked into the back of his waistband. He visibly tensed and with parted lips, I watched as the calm façade slip right off his face. He sucked in a sharp breath, and I glided my palm over his bulge with the intention of having him fuck me right there.

I tried not to let my eyes widen with surprise at how painfully hard he must have been.

"The—" he muttered, swallowing hard and I watched the desperation float off him. "Fuck, Nova. Are you trying to kill me?"

"No," I said, slightly frowning and smirking. "Why would I do that?"

He chuckled, shaking his head. Ramiro's hands on my thighs tightened, denting into my skin and I watched as he spread my legs further. When he stared up at me, the light pouring down on us hit him in a different way. His eyes weren't brown. They were green. A deep and forest green hidden by dark and thick lashes. So devilishly beautiful.

I felt his fingertips slide against the inside of my thigh, dangerously close to the spot I wanted him the most.

"You don't care?" he asked, tracing the front of my underwear with his fingers.

I bit my lip, swallowing as he glided over my covered clit. No, I didn't care. I'd never see him again. I shook my head and his fingers slipped underneath the material.

I wanted him. I wanted the memory of him. He touched my hole and his reaction was bigger than mine. I gasped, but his eyes fluttered shut as he felt how wet I was for him. His jaw ticked, desperation and lust morphing into one expression on his face. It was a sight I didn't want to look away from.

He sighed, kissing the corner of my mouth. "God, you're so fucking beautiful."

I liked the compliment. I didn't like how slow he was taking it.

Ramiro opened his eyes again and for the first time that night, I felt the need to push him away. Not out of fear. He wanted me and the only thing that scared me was how eager I was for it.

"Am I moving too slow for you, Nova?" he asked as if he had read me like an open book. Was I that obvious? I nodded anyway. I was aching. I was extremely bothered, and it didn't help that Ramiro wanted to take his time with me.

"Yeah?" he breathed, kissing over my collarbones. "I'm just enjoying you."

"Shit," I stammered, feeling his fingertips loop over the front of my dress. With a gentle tug, my breasts were open to his view.

He let out a guttural moan and with furrowed brows, he leaned down and caught my nipple with his lips. I didn't have time to think about the way I looked to him. His face conveyed the message.

I groaned, feeling his tongue slide over my nipple while his hand roamed the other. How could it feel that good? He enjoyed it too. Ramiro sighed, closing his eyes when he sucked on my skin.

"You smell so fucking good," he whispered huskily, his palm covering one of my tits.

My heart pounded in my ears, but I ignored it. I ignored how the pulsing of my pussy matched my heartbeat. Despite wishing he'd slide into me, I didn't want whatever he was doing to end.

"Fuck," I gasped out, my head falling back. He sucked and kissed on my breasts, moulding me in his hands as if he didn't want to let go. I didn't want him to.

I was quickly overwhelmed by the amount of pleasure soaring through me, and it confused me. It was my fucking chest. How could it feel as if as I could orgasm from that alone?

Ramiro kissed a line from my cleavage to my neck, eventually stopping underneath my ear. I supressed a violent shiver from racking through me.

"Are you going to let me taste you now, Nova?" he whispered, letting his teeth graze over my lobe.

What on earth did I get myself into? I watched him, observing the sheer willingness on his face. Instead of giving him a verbal answer, I leaned back on my palms and lifted my hips. Ramiro smirked and ran his hands over my thighs, catching the material of my underwear and exposing me to his view.

"Ramiro," I whispered, the urge cover myself too strong to ignore.

He gripped my jaw in one hand, forcing an eye contact I almost shied away from. "Are you going to let me fuck you with my tongue, hermosa?"

Yes.

My chest heaved with short, unsteady breaths. He slid his thumb over my jaw, leaving a path of fire wherever he touched. He must have seen how badly I wanted it. Ramiro stared at me, silently daring me to answer and I let the word fall from my lips without a care in the world.

"Yes."

He grinned, letting go of me. "Good girl."

I barely had time to think about my response, or his own. Ramiro fell to his knees, lowering himself. On the table, my pussy was open to his view—eye level with his face. I nearly closed my legs, but Ramiro licked his lips and stared at me as if I were on the dinner menu.

His gaze didn't stray, nor did his hands. He watched me and with each passing second, the utter need in his eyes grew. His breathing noticeably quickened as he ran the tip of his nose along the inside of my thigh, still looking at my most intimate part with enough lust to fuck for days.

"You look so beautiful like this," he said, his voice soft and hoarse.

I can't wait anymore.

I moaned, letting my head roll back as he sucked the flesh on my thigh. He closed his eyes, groaning as if I were the one pleasuring him. When he kissed me on the clit, I wasn't ready for it. I gasped, surprised by the feeling of a warm and wet mouth surrounding me.

Ramiro moaned with me, his eyes closed. Holy shit. I frowned, trying to control my breathing as I stared at the top of his dark hair. He gripped my thigh, hoisting it over his shoulder as he held me wide open for him.

I was about to burst.

"Fuck," he drawled, pulling back to give my pussy one last look. It didn't last long. Ramiro delved forward again, sucking on my clit as if his life depended on it.

Nothing about me had calmed down. Nothing about me was relaxed. I was entirely too tense from pleasure and I felt my back meet the table, losing the ability to keep myself up anymore.

"Miro," I whispered out, barely realising I had shortened his name.

He smiled against me, loving the nickname. Or was he just amused at how good he was making me feel?

I moved, overwhelmed by all the sensations I was feeling. I thought about how Ramiro was a stranger, and I stopped thinking about it almost immediately. It didn't matter. He was on his knees for me, pleasuring me because he wanted to.

Using two fingers, he spread my slit and ran a flat, heavy tongue over my pussy. I was drenched and he tasted me, moaning out loud when he did so.

It was too much for me to take. Is that what it feels like? I never imagined that anything could feel that way.

"Nova?" Ramiro called out my name.

"Yes?" Why was my own voice barely recognisable?

"Move one more fucking time," he said, staring up at me with the threat in his words loud and clear.

I stilled instantly, swallowing hard and obeying his demands. His eyes stayed on my face and I scowled in pleasure, finding the way his tongue traced my pussy a sight too erotic.

I still had my heels on. My dress was under my tits. I could only imagine how flushed I was.

He tightened his hold on me, holding me steady when he slowly started sliding his tongue into me. Shit. There was no way I could take that. I squirmed, trying to ease the amount of adrenaline pumping through my veins and quickly realised my mistake.

"Ramiro," I gasped, watching as he let go of me.

He stood up and I let out a small yelp when he pulled me to my feet, the look on his face stoic. I nearly stumbled in my heels, but Ramiro bent down and closed his arms around my thighs.

"Ramiro," I said his name, but I was thrown over his shoulder while he ignored me.

He started walking.

"Miro," I breathed out, feeling his hand give me a small slap on my bare ass.

Even that feels good.

My heart was erratic in my chest as I let him take me wherever he wanted. I gulped, still reeling over the remnants of kisses between my thighs. Why did he stop? I almost yelled at him—I almost demanded that he take the both of us back to that table. I didn't.

The way he held me and carried me, I knew Ramiro was not done with me. On the contrary.

"Where are you taking me?" I asked, my voice soft and wary.

"My bedroom."

Chapter 4

I didn't know what to expect nor did I have a single clue on what I was getting myself into. It didn't matter because Ramiro was about to show me.

He carried me, holding me steady and I watched the floor beneath us move.

I could still feel him between my thighs. I could still feel his tongue, and his hands on me. I was full of complaints and I nearly voiced them out loud. How dare he edge me? How dare he stop making me feel good? I almost laughed at my utter desperation for the release he started and ended when I wasn't ready for it to.

Was I ever in control? Surely he was lying when he said that.

The floor changed, and I realised too late that we were in his room. My front met the mattress, and I was caught off guard.

I didn't have time to register that I was on his bed before he gripped my waist, roughly turning me onto my back instead. I took my first deep breath in, staring up at Ramiro and the way he loomed over me.

It was precisely in that moment when I felt encaged—trapped by a man who looked as if he could fuck me into tomorrow.

Ramiro peered down at me, cocking his head to the side. I opened my mouth, but a strong hand around my ankle shut me up quickly. He dragged me to the edge and my legs were spread, opening me up to his view. I didn't resist. I couldn't.

I looked up at the ceiling, breathing through my nose when I felt him undo the straps on my heels. Damn it.

"Ramiro—"

I choked on air, startled by Ramiro sliding a wet and warm tongue over my clit. Fuck, I wasn't expecting that. He gripped the inside of my knees, forcing my thighs to my chest and I let him move me as he pleased.

I was a mess, and Ramiro didn't stop there.

Was that supposed to be my punishment?

His hand glided over my stomach, reaching over my chest until it wrapped around the front of my throat. Ramiro tightened his hand, holding me down and I felt myself liking it a little too much. I grasped at his forearm—the only thing within my reach and I wasn't pushing him away.

I didn't see his smile but I felt it on my skin.

He traced his tongue over my pussy, circling over my clit and I lifted my head to watch him. I need to see him. With his eyes already on my face, I found myself enjoying the way his tongue flicked over my clit. It was too much. I could barely breathe as I soaked in the sight of Ramiro enjoying me.

His gaze was dangerously soft, half lidded and absolutely fixated on me. The intention of having me cum was written all over his fucking face. I was his for the night and he knew it.

I breathed out a pleasured sigh and his hand around my neck tightened, reminding me that I was completely at his will. Losing all sense of doubt, I widened my legs for the man between them.

His mouth closed around my clit, his own moan sending vibrations through me. Ramiro sucked, and I glanced at him to find his eyes peacefully closed. He fucking loves it.

My head fell back and I let go of his arm, completely fascinated by the amount of pleasure his tongue could give me.

"Fuck, Nova," he groaned, running a smooth and gentle hand along the inside of my thigh. It was followed by his kisses. With parted lips, Ramiro adorned my skin with pecks and words in a language I couldn't understand.

He ran his nose along my skin, breathing in deeply and I thought about how I'd never experienced such adoration before. It was new—a feeling I'd remember when we parted ways. His hand left my throat and I wanted it back. I missed it already.

"You're so pretty," he whispered, his brows furrowed when he kissed my hole. "You're so fucking pretty."

He slid both hands underneath my ass and squeezed me, letting out a small moan when he did so. Ramiro almost seemed like he was on the receiving end. He made it seem as if he loved making me feel good.

I let out a groan, feeling myself clench around nothing. I wanted more. I wanted him to fuck me in the position I was already in.

"Ramiro," I moaned his name, uncaring of how it sounded. I ran my hand over his full head of dark hair, intertwining my fingers through it. His response was a tongue through my slit, unbearably slow and it drove me insane.

Fuck. My eyes squeezed shut, wincing as an orgasm started in the pit of my stomach.

Ramiro kissed my clit, and I held my breath when he didn't do it again. I almost screamed at him. His breath fanned against me and I tensed, hoping he'd put me out of my misery and he didn't. His kisses were laid on my thighs, and my chest heaved when I realised how close I was.

My stomach clenched and I ran my tongue over my lips, forcing myself to be quiet.

He wanted me to ask for it.

The tip of his tongue went slowly over my clit and I grunted, clenching my eyes shut. I was wet—utterly soaked. My thighs were around his head and I stared down at him, finding a patient look on his face. He could do this all night.

His hands didn't stop roaming my body. He held me, squeezed me and soothed the pain with his palms. It was too much, and too little.

Ramiro smirked, kissing me over my skin and missing all the spots I wanted him at the most. I reached my hand down, desperate for any sort of friction but his fingers around my wrist stopped me.

I could barely focus on how quick he was to catch me.

Shit. Was that my punishment? The fucking teasing? I breathed in deeply through my nose, fighting through the feeling of my orgasm coming and going. His lips barely touching me drove me to the edge and I felt all sense of vanity slip straight from my grasp.

"Ramiro," I gasped out, sliding my hands over his head. "Please."

"Please?" he repeated. "I didn't think you were one for begging, Nova."

"Fuck," I cussed, barely able to contain myself. He dragged his hand over my stomach, finding my breast in his palm and I heard him let out a soft noise.

Ramiro's mouth wasn't touching anymore. I could feel his breath. I could feel his hands running along my skin. It felt good, but it wasn't what I needed and I almost begged for more. My body was hot, tortured by his hindrance.

"Miro," I whispered his name as if I had done it a million times before.

"Yes, hermosa?"

I ran my tongue over my teeth, swallowing hard.

"I'm listening," he murmured softly, kissing my lower stomach.

"I won't move again," I breathed. "Please. I swear."

His lips pulled up into a smirk, and I knew that I had said the exact words he wanted to hear. My stomach clenched, agony and need flowing through me in waves. Fucker.

"Good girl," he whispered, giving me an open mouth kiss on my clit.

He travelled lower, roaming my pussy with his tongue until it slipped inside of me. I groaned, arching my back off the bed when he started thrusting his tongue in and out of me.

That mouth.

I couldn't think straight. I was completely, and utterly hooked on the way Ramiro was making me feel. He moaned, shifting his jaw and I felt him push deeper. He wanted all of me. He wanted to taste all of me.

My lips fell apart when he flicked his tongue, hitting a spot that had my hands curling into fists.

When his thumb started circling my clit, I knew I was done for.

I had been on the edge of an orgasm since he started but right then, I came harder than I ever came before.

"Fuck," he groaned, swirling his tongue around and I let my hand weave through his hair. "You taste so fucking good, Nova. Fuck—I can't stop. I don't want to stop."

Is that part of the reason why he didn't want me to come?

"Ramiro," I moaned out loud, closing my eyes as he tongue fucked me straight into an orgasm. It was...indescribable. I could hardly breathe.

Ramiro was relentless, squeezing my thighs while I came so hard my body went rigid. I gazed down, watching his tongue slide in and out of me and run along my clit before thrusting into me again. I lost count on how many times I came. It was one after the next and Ramiro didn't stop.

I felt my eyes water, overwhelmed by the amount of pleasure rushing through me. I stuck to my promise, staying unmoving even when it felt as if I couldn't take it anymore.

"Oh, fuck," I groaned, feeling every muscle in my body tensing as he licked me all the way from my hole to my clit. It was at that point when it, truly, became too much. I couldn't comprehend a sensible thought.

All I could think of was; is this how an orgasm is supposed to feel like?

He must have known that I was spent. With one more kiss, he pulled away and I felt myself sink into the mattress.

Breathing heavy, I reached for him and he didn't hesitate.

I grabbed the sides of his head, kissing him on his swollen and red lips.

"Good?" he breathed out, smiling against me and I almost scoffed at the stupid question. Yes.

"Yes," I whispered, still trying to catch my breath. Even after that, I wanted more than just his mouth and I wanted it immediately.

I started unbuckling his belt and he let me, watching me with a gaze far too intense to look at. He was hard, unbelievably fucking hard. It strained against his pants, and I wondered how he managed to endure that. Surely it wasn't comfortable.

"Are you going to fuck me now?" I murmured, kneeling on the bed while I unbuttoned his shirt. Ramiro pulled his bottom lip into his mouth, and I smirked when more tattooed and tanned skin came to view. He was...better than I expected.

I wanted to see all of him.

My knees still felt weak, almost on the verge of collapsing under me and yet, I craved more. I wanted his orgasm on me, or in me or whatever the fuck his heart desired.

He leaned closer, kissing me on the shoulder and I dragged the shirt off his body. I ran my fingers over the indents on his stomach, feeling his muscles flex underneath my touch. He's almost shaking.

"Nervous?" I whispered, hearing his breath tremble.

Nothing. I looked up at him, seeing his throat moving as he swallowed. Oh? He was? My eyes stayed on him for a second longer. He wasn't hiding how he felt.

"Don't be," I said softly, running my hand over his chest. "You're in control."

His eyes flicked to mine. "Yeah?"

"Yeah."

Ramiro was the hottest man I've ever seen. There was no question about it. I'd let him do anything to me if it felt good enough.

His arms were inked all the way down to the back of his hands and I traced a certain tattoo on his ribs with the tips of my fingers. Of course I'd want him to feel as if he didn't need to hold back.

Of course.

"When are you going to take this dress off, huh?" he asked quietly, his fingers toying with the ends of my curls when he locked eyes with me.

I looked down, forgetting that I'd been in a dress that covered absolutely nothing. At the same time I went to unzip my dress, Ramiro reached for his belt and I watched him pull it from its constraint.

My heart beat in my ears as I got rid of my dress, exposing myself to Ramiro and his predatory gaze.

He breathed in deeply and his jaw ticked, the unquestionable lust on his face growing the longer he looked at me. It was the kind of lust I didn't hate. It was the kind that made me feel as if he really fucking wanted me. Not for just his own pleasure, but for mine too.

He undid the button on his pants and I watched with a pounding heart. When his boxers fell, so did my jaw. Fuck. I ran my tongue over my lower lip, wondering if I could take all of him. I reached out to him, yearning to feel him in my palm but Ramiro caught my hand.

He bent down, his eyes flickering between my own and I was enchanted by the dark green staring straight back at me.

"The first time you touch me," he murmured slowly, "is when I'm inside of you."

As much as I wanted to protest, I didn't.

He ran his thumb over my lips, sighing as his gaze followed his strokes.

"You're so fucking beautiful, Nova," he breathed out, and I saw the exact moment something in his gaze changed. He kissed me, and stole my breath in the process.

It wasn't like our other kisses. It was deep, rushed and I felt his tongue against mine. It was a real fucking kiss—the type of kiss you'd think about on a loop days after. It made my pussy violently throb, nearly begging for Ramiro's to fuck me as if it was life or death.

I moaned out loud, and his hand sunk into my hair to grab a fistful. It didn't hurt but fuck, I almost wanted it to. I was breathless, feeling Ramiro suck on my tongue and close a hand around the front of my throat.

I was in his hands and he knew how to work me. He knew as if I wasn't a stranger he met a few hours ago. Ramiro tightened his hand around my neck and used the other to grab my cheeks, forcing me to look up at him.

"Open this mouth," he whispered, staring down at me. "And fucking kiss me, Nova."

"Fuck," I murmured, sliding my hand over the back of his head. I opened for him and my tongue slipped past his lips, feeling his moan run through him.

I didn't hold back, and he didn't either.

When was the last time I was kissed like that? I couldn't remember. It was eager. It was messy. And I fucking loved it.

With his lips on mine, I felt his hands grip at my waist. He lifted me off my knees with an ease I couldn't understand and I fell to my back. He was on top of me instantly, holding himself up on the palms of his hands and I was beneath him.

Ramiro groaned, sucking my bottom lip into his mouth and finishing it off with a gentle tug of his teeth.

He's a good kisser.

My head hit his pillow, engulfed by the scent of him. I hooked my legs around his waist, and his dick hit the inside of my thigh. I was irrevocably ready for him.

I sighed, running my hand over his back and when he buried his head in my neck, I saw a tattoo I didn't see before. It was huge and took up most of his back, covering his skin with dark ink and intricate designs. There was one behind his ear too. How did I manage to miss that?

His back was one of the hottest things about him.

"Nova?" he breathed, and I felt the tip of his dick nudge right where I wanted him.

"Yes, Miro," I panted. "Yes."

As soon as the words left my mouth, Ramiro sunk into me.

I let out a small scream, completely filled by him as he stretched me out. Nothing has ever felt that good. Nothing could compare. He slid into me and he gasped into my ear, his lips barely grazing my skin.

I felt my eyes roll back when he inched deeper, making me take every single part of him and for a moment, I was stunned by the amount of pleasure flowing through me. Shit. I groaned, feeling a shiver dance along my skin.

I couldn't speak. I couldn't get a single word out. He felt exactly as I thought he would.

No, it was better.

"Fuck," he grunted, pushing himself impossibly deeper. "You fe el...fucking unbelievable, Nova."

I held onto him, bracing myself when he thrust into me again and I stopped breathing for a second. My arousal dripped around him and I didn't care. I was wet for him and he took advantage of it, sliding in and out of me with a pace I struggled to keep up with.

He kissed the side of my neck, filling me up completely and I let my pussy squeeze around him. Ramiro's response was a deep groan—one that came straight from his chest and I chased the sound. I loved the noises he made.

He gripped the inside of my thigh and I felt him open me up wider, slipping in deeper and staying there. My moans didn't stop. It echoed through his room.

"Feel that, Nova?" he breathed. "Do you feel how deep I am? Say you want more."

There's more?

"More," I gasped out with no hesitation. It didn't feel like I could take more, but I blurted the word and regret didn't follow.

Ramiro held my hip, holding me steady when he finally allowed me to feel all of him and I couldn't help but let out a small cry. It was intense. He thrust into me and kissed the shell of my ear, fucking me in the middle of his mattress while I completely lost myself.

"I can't get enough of you," he whimpered, his own resolution hanging by a thread.

I was sensitive. I was on the brink of another orgasm. Ramiro reached under me and squeezed my ass, slapping my skin while he rolled his hips.

I was a mess underneath him. His chest was against mine, trapping me and I couldn't fault it. I liked the feeling. I could run my nails along his back and enjoy his shivers.

His lips found mine, catching my breath and making it his own. I tightened my legs around his waist, bringing him closer even when the space between us didn't exist.

My pussy took all of him and as wet as I was, Ramiro stretched me in a way that felt unfamiliar. He was unrelenting and his dick was incredibly hard. I could almost feel him pulsing inside of me. With one last kiss, Ramiro pulled out of me.

The look in his eyes was unrecognisable—something along the lines of I can't stop fucking you. I took a deep breath in, composing myself but he held my waist and turned me onto my stomach. With his hands holding my hips, Ramiro forced me to my knees and I caught myself on my hands.

He was quick to take his place again, thrusting inside of me.

"You make me feel so good," I whispered, glancing back to find his head thrown back. He held my hips, fucking me hard and unforgivingly.

He was merciless, bruising my skin and I welcomed the pain. It opened up a whole new world for me—one that I didn't think I'd like but there I was, arching my back for him and wishing he'd see how much I enjoyed it.

His eyes met mine. "You have no idea how you make me feel. No fucking idea."

I can see, and feel. Ramiro didn't stop moving. He pounded into me, holding my waist and I let out a strangled cry when his pace quickened. He was harsh, and I took it. He was brutal and I welcomed it. At the same time, it felt as if he was waiting for me to cum first and I did.

A moan escaped my throat, unstoppable and loud. Everything in my body clenched and I heard Ramiro's reaction, finding it impossible to keep myself from cumming right on his dick.

It came in waves. My orgasm had the both of us groaning, and I squeezed my eyes shut when my hand went to my lower stomach.

Fuck. How much more could I possibly take?

If Ramiro wasn't holding me, I would have collapsed onto my stomach ages ago. I rode out my climax, reaching the end with breathless moans and distorted noises.

My orgasm finished, and it lit the fuse for Ramiro's own orgasm.

"Hermosa," he groaned, his voice strained. "I'm cumming."

He quickened his pace, thrusting into me hard and with a second to spare, Ramiro slipped out of me. He released himself all over my ass and I watched him stroke himself, the sight too erotic to not enjoy. With a thrown back head, small noises came from his throat and my gaze travelled down to his tense abdomen.

I was spent—completely and utterly fucked.

I looked at Ramiro and his gaze met mine, a similar look on the both of our face. Satisfied. He leaned down and planted a kiss on my shoulder, getting off the bed.

"Don't move, Nova," he told me, his voice thick and his skin glistening with a sheer layer of sweet. "I'll get something to clean you up."

I fell onto my stomach, still breathing heavy as I laid there. I didn't know if I'd ever see Ramiro again. I knew that even if we parted ways, he was undeniably and certainly going to be engraved into my memory.

And just like that, our night together ended as soon as it started.

Chapter 5

"Is it okay if I fuck you for the rest of the night?" he whispered, his breath fanning over my jawline. "Is it okay if I taste you until you stop me?"

I could barely speak. I could barely catch my breath.

My moans escaped freely and I closed my eyes, lost in the feeling of Ramiro inside of me. He wasn't moving anymore. I was in a daze and he was on top of me, hard and warm and still.

He made me feel all of him. He made me take all of him. And it was impossible not to like it.

I sighed dreamily, feeling Ramiro kiss my neck as if he were obsessed with me—as if he couldn't get enough of me. There wasn't a moment he wasn't touching me.

How could anything feel that good?

He moaned my name and whispered how good it felt for him, his voice hoarse and breathless. I saw stars. Quick fuck? No, it wasn't. I lost count of the amount of times we came.

I lost count of the amount of times he slipped out of me and had his head between my thighs. He had me in the palm of his hand and I couldn't complain.

The only complaint I had was that we started so late.

I didn't want our night to end and he didn't either. He'd clean me up, and I'd have him back once again. Just as I thought I was about to leave, he'd reel me right back in. I was easy, but so was he.

"Nova," he whimpered, his brows furrowed and his eyes soft. "I don't want to stop having you."

"Then don't," I murmured, sliding my hand over his back. I didn't care that the sun might come up soon. Or that I was going to be sore. My legs were around his waist and he took me, making me his even if it was just for the night.

"Yeah?" he murmured, sliding his nose over the skin on my neck. He breathed in and let out a sigh, a little moan falling from his lips.

"Yeah," I said, my head falling back when I felt him lower himself down my body for the countless time.

And he had me until dawn broke.

He had me until we tired ourselves out.

It took a while for my legs to start working, and for the high he gave me to simmer away. Even then, I was walking on clouds and Ramiro was the cause of it.

He let me use his shower, and offered a clean t-shirt that smelled like his pillows. All with a smile on his face. He watched me and I let him, enjoying the look on his face when I stood naked in front him.

How could he look at me like even after he got what he wanted?

Afterwards, I fell asleep on his bed but that wasn't my intention. I was never planning on staying, but Ramiro pulled me close to him and my body allowed me to dose off in the position he put me in.

It was a night that followed me into my dreams.

The next morning, I woke up before he did.

He slept on his back with the sheets at his waist, his hair messy and his face peaceful. He was in a deep sleep, his lips parted as his chest slowly fell and raised.

If I could have taken a picture of him, I would've.

His skin was covered in my marks but I didn't look any better. I had the memory of him temporarily etched onto me, but he did too. My nails might have scratched him a bit harder than I thought, and I might have kissed his skin harsher than I intended. He didn't complain, on the contrary.

It looked good next to his tattoos and I stared at him while he showered.

Ten minutes after I woke up, I was gone.

I didn't want to leave. I didn't want to overstay, either. It was a situation I didn't want to be in—the awkwardness of waking up together as if we weren't strangers to each other.

Perhaps I was wrong, but I didn't wait to find out how he felt about me still being there when he stirred out of his sleep.

But I did almost wake him up when I struggled to find a missing earring, my shoes and my handbag. Eventually leaving the earring, I found my shoes and handbag on two far ends of his house and I couldn't fathom how that happened.

There wasn't a room we didn't fuck in and in the cab drive back to my car, I thought about all the ways he made me feel.

It stayed on my mind even long after my marks have left, and I had nothing but the t-shirt he borrowed me and a long daydream that occupied my thoughts.

That was two weeks ago.

"Why do you have so much shit?" Ethan huffed out, dropping a box that clearly had fragile written on it.

I looked at my brother and sighed, annoyed that I bothered to ask for his help.

If a moving van didn't cost and an arm and a leg, he wouldn't even have known that I was moving across the city. I stared at him, watching as he placed two hands on his hips and take a deep breath in.

I swear if he didn't have a helpful van...

"What?" he asked, that familiar dumb look his face.

All I could do was shake my head at him.

"What?" he asked again, a scowl on his forehead.

It was hard to forget that Ethan was my younger brother. He always acted like it. He was also the family favourite—or he used to be when my mother still roamed the earth.

Ethan wasn't as dumb as he looked. He was the adored one with sports achievements from one corner of the world to the next. My parents loved me, a lot and almost too much, but Ethan was the baby who came two years after me. He was honest and kind and I was the older sister who made him that way—as my parents would say.

Honest and kind? Well, he kind of used to be.

"You have a lot of shit, Nova," he complained again, rolling his eyes and turning to face the view. "What made you choose this place, anyway?"

I shrugged, "It's nice, isn't it?"

The real reason was that it was cheaper. I was already living above my means before I was fired and the only option was to downgrade to a cute place in a town Ethan called sketchy.

It wasn't—and it was.

On the top floor, I had a view of the city below. Tall buildings took up most of the place, but I didn't care.

Ethan slowly turned to me, pursing his lips. "As long as you're happy."

"You're so annoying," I muttered, using a box-cutter to slice through the thick brown tape on one of my boxes.

It had my shoes in, and I caught a glimpse of the ones Ramiro took off me. I hadn't stopped thinking about him and I almost regretted leaving without saying goodbye. Almost.

I knew where he lived. I wasn't going to do anything about it, but I knew where he lived.

"I'm annoying?" he said, flicking through a book he found. "You have me up and down these stairs with heavy boxes and I'm the annoying one?"

I, absolutely, regretted asking him for help. I threw a decorative pillow at his face, hearing his shocked gasp echoed through my empty apartment once it hit him on the forehead. He laughed, and placed it back down on the plastic covered couch.

I cracked a smile too, shaking my head when he started unpacking with me. Ethan complained, but he always pulled through for me. It was a trait he got from our dad. He mumbled and sighed and got the job done without further questions.

It was part of the reason I bothered to ask him in the first place.

I looked around, already feeling defeated by the amount of boxes scattered around. It was going to take forever to unpack and I groaned, holding a hand to my forehead. It's already night.

"We're missing a box," I muttered, eyeing the floor. "Must still be in your van."

I looked up just in time to find Ethan flinging his keys into my direction, a cheeky look on his face. I caught it, glaring at him when he nodded in approval. Brothers.

Why couldn't my sweet mother bless me with a sweet sister? I probably cried for one as a child.

"It's your turn to walk," he said, grabbing the box cutter from my hand.

I wiped my hands and headed to the door, leaving Ethan to sort out the mess I could hardly stand to look at. I was tired, but I grabbed my hoodie on the way out and closed the door behind me.

The only thing I didn't like of the place was the amount of time it took to get outside. It was a long walk down a hallway until the stairs leading to the ground floor and a quick walk through the foyer. It felt safe, but at the same time—was it really?

I avoided the elevator at all costs. I didn't like the tightness of it and I couldn't whine about it not working. I wasn't going to use it anyway.

I dragged my feet over the flight of stairs, eventually reaching the floor.

Ethan's van was parked outside and I opened the backdoors, finding the box I'd forgotten in the corner. I stepped up into the van, half irritated that it was dark and I couldn't see anything. I found it and kept it up on one hand, holding the keys in the other. I stepped out, closing the doors and making sure it was locked.

Now for the walk back.

At least the box wasn't heavy.

I walked through the foyer for the millionth time that day with the cardboard box in my arms. I was already sick of it. All I wanted to do was lie down on my bed and wish my things would magically be in their place the next day.

Ethan is probably breaking a few of my things. With that thought in my mind, I started walking a little bit faster than before.

"Nova?"

At the sound of my name, I turned around.

I didn't expect to come face to face with Ramiro, and I felt my heart drop straight to my ass. Why? I don't know.

I locked eyes with him, and a small smile spread across his lips as if he were happy to see me. Was it insane of me to believe that I'd never run into Ramiro again?

The city was big but there he was two weeks later in the apartment building I'd just moved into. What were the fucking chances? I gazed around, noting his familiar sports car standing outside that I, somehow, didn't notice before.

"Ramiro," I murmured, shifting the box in my arm for a better grip.

His smile widened, reaching his eyes and I watched those dimples I couldn't forget. What was wrong with me? I needed to get back to Ethan.

I couldn't stand there and look at the man who fucked me into the mattress. No, I couldn't. I was hit with flashbacks and it was unbearable.

"Do you live here?" he asked curiously, his dark eyes fixated on me. His body was covered by casual clothes—a white t-shirt and a grey sweatpants. He looked...good. Some of his tattoos were covered, but I noticed a fading scratch on the side of his neck and I knew it was the one I accidently gave him.

"I do now," I answered, letting my tongue run over my lower lip. "What are you doing here?"

"I'm visiting someone," he said, his eyes darting up the stairs.

That voice. Visiting someone.

His gaze dropped back to mine, and he asked the question I already saw on his face, "Is it okay if I walk you to your apartment?"

Chapter 6

"You feel so perfect," he breathed, a small whimper in his voice. "How do you feel so perfect?"

"Miro," I moaned his name and felt his lips on my back, kissing my skin. "I can't."

"Yes, hermosa," he whispered, running his tongue along my neck. "Yes, you can."

I looked at Ramiro, and found it hard to say no to him. How could I? It was just a walk back to my door and he wasn't coming inside. Again. I nearly cracked a smile, but I nodded when I started walking back to my place.

"Of course," I said despite the warning sirens blaring off in my head.

Bad idea.

Or was it?

He reminded me that I was easy, and I didn't know if I liked the way it felt or not. Ramiro followed with me, and I wasn't going to allow the pounding of my heart to shake me when I felt him next to me. His presence was suffocating. There has to be something wrong with me.

How could he have so much power? It had been two weeks. Shouldn't I have forgotten about him by now? Wasn't he supposed to forget about me?

"Thank you," I muttered, feeling Ramiro take the box from my hands and hold it in his own.

He offered a small smile, but there was a glint in his eye that didn't go unnoticed. I couldn't read it, and I wasn't sure if I wanted to.

"No problem, Nova," he said softly, and I spared him a quick glance.

He wasn't smiling anymore. He was stoic—completely unreadable. He looked down at the floor and I watched his jaw tick. No problem, Nova? I ran my tongue over my teeth and ignored it, finding the tension in my body almost too much to handle. He wasn't even doing anything.

The both us starting moving up the stairs, and my gaze dropped to his tattooed hands. Every part of him reminded me of something that happened that night. It was odd. I could feel him between my thighs, and I hated that I thought about it every time I looked at him.

He was a stranger who had seen me in every position possible.

Did that make him a stranger? No, I wanted to invite him in and have a rerun. I wasn't going to, but I could think about it.

Oh, I forgot Ethan is here.

He walked alongside me, not saying a single word. I didn't let it affect me, or show that it did. Why would I? He was only walking me to my apartment.

We eventually reached my door, and I almost let out a sigh of relief. There was a note taped on the wooden door, clearly in Ethan's capitalised handwriting and I felt my face drop.

I'll be back in thirty minutes. Key is somewhere you can't reach.

Fucker.

The note was ended with Ethan's attempt at a tongue-out face and I stared at the paper with the sharpest glare I could muster. Ethan was a pain in my neck. He probably got bored and decided to wander off to one of his friends that lived nearby.

He also thought it'd be a good idea to advertise that my key was somewhere close by.

He just...doesn't think.

"Boyfriend?" Ramiro asked, a slight frown on his forehead.

He stared at the paper, an almost...concerned look on his face. Or it was something else. I didn't look long enough to find out but I didn't miss that he played with his fingers as if he were stopping himself. From what? I couldn't say.

I shook my head. "No. Brother."

His dark eyes met mine, and I found myself thinking of all the ways he looked up at me. Stop. I needed to get away from him.

Ramiro nodded and his hands visibly relaxed when he silently reached up to the doorframe. I watched his bare arm flex and I let my gaze trace over the ink on his skin. He didn't need to stretch to reach, but the bottom of his t-shirt lifted and I saw those v-lines I had to look away from.

Fuck.

He felt around and grabbed the small key, an annoyed look on his face when his arm fell back down. We were both annoyed, but he seemed a little bit more than me.

"Okay," he nodded, staring at the key between his fingertips. "He just left this here? Smart of him."

The sarcasm was loud. I couldn't disagree.

Ethan should've waited the two minutes it took for me to get back if he wanted to leave.

"Well," I shrugged, opening my palm and accepting the key he held out for me. I unlocked my door, finding the place empty and just as I left it.

Don't invite him in.

I turned to Ramiro, and he probably didn't even know how hard I was contemplating having him step inside for a moment. I didn't know why I felt compelled to. The thought of being alone with him shouldn't have been as frightening as it was. Or as tempting as it was.

"Ramiro," I murmured, and he must have seen the look on my face.

"I'll be good, Nova," he murmured, his voice gentle. "I swear."

He knew what I was thinking. He wanted to come inside too. I sucked my lower lip and watched Ramiro's eyes drop to my mouth. This time, the look on his face was all too readable. I pushed the door wider, stepping inside and feeling Ramiro's presence behind me.

"Come."

The door shut, and the clear sound of the lock being pushed into place echoed through my empty flat. Like the first time I heard him lock a door, my heart raced out of my chest.

"Right here?" he asked, setting the box down on one of the only open spots on the floor.

"I'm sorry about the mess, I'm still in the middle of unpacking," I murmured, feeling my lips pull up into a small smile. "Thank you for walking with me."

"Don't worry about it," he said, his accented voice low.

He stepped closer, and I let my eyes follow his. Ramiro was intimidating in every way but his cologne had to be the most inviting smell ever. I wanted him closer, and he did exactly so. I got a better look at him, but it took all the strength I had to stop myself from glancing lower.

All of it.

He breathed out a sigh and I felt his hand on my cheek, the feel of him hitting me in all the right spots. The morning I left, I almost turned back around. I wanted more than I already got and I felt selfish because of it.

Looking back now, I wished I stayed to find out how he felt about me still being there when he stirred out of his sleep.

There wasn't humour in his eyes when he looked at me. Or playfulness. Ramiro stared at me as if he had a question and it was one he desperately needed the answer to.

"Pretty," he whispered, and I felt his palm run over my shoulder. "Why did you leave before I got the chance to say goodbye to you?"

Is that why he was ticked off? I couldn't say anything. I didn't have an answer. It was supposed to be a quick fuck and I almost told him that. It was anything but.

We talked, too. We didn't know each other but we had a conversation that made me feel like we did. His laugh was infectious but in that moment, Ramiro's dimpled smile was nowhere on his face.

He wasn't pleased. Was I? I wish I were the confident version of myself I was that night.

"Nova," he said my name and I locked eyes with him, every part of my body warming up.

Why does he have to be attractive?

"You promised you'll be good," I said quietly, my eyes drifting to the door. What did good even mean? Did it mean he shouldn't touch me? I had no objections if he wanted to.

His hand ran over my arm and I held back a shiver. As if the memories lied underneath his fingertips, I was hit with vivid images and I almost cussed myself for it.

Shut the fuck up.

"This is me being good," Ramiro said, his brows pinching together.

I let out a small laugh, "I have a hard time believing that."

"Hermosa," he whispered, his hand curling into mine when he planted a kiss on my knuckles. "Imagine how I felt when the woman I thought I'd wake up next to was gone."

"Imagine how I felt when I realised I had no way of contacting her." He leaned down and I swallowed, closing my eyes when his familiar lips kissed the side of my neck. "Or that I knew nothing of her except her name and the place she used to work at. Am I fucking insane, Nova? For thinking I'd be able to get you out of my head?"

"Miro," I murmured, my hand on his chest but I was never planning on pushing him away. "It was one fucking night."

"I know," he breathed, and I was entranced by the lips grazing over my jaw. "I know it was. I wish it was more."

I did, too. I didn't have it in me to say it out loud. In my apartment with nothing but bubble wrap and boxes littering the floor, I wished we were back in Ramiro's house with his hand about to lock the door.

I struggled to understand how I could be that attracted to him. He fucked me good and that was it. It shouldn't have been more than that. Ever.

"You're all I've been thinking about," he said, his tone gentle when his hand touched my waist. "I lied to you, Nova. I'm sorry."

I stopped and stared up at him, my voice wary when I spoke, "about what?"

I imagined the worst. I imagined that he was about to tell he killed people with the gun he pulled from his pants. I imagined that he was about to tell me his name wasn't Ramiro and that wasn't his home.

I felt my heart throb and it left an unnerving feeling spiralling through me.

"I wasn't visiting anyone," he said, unknowingly putting me out of my misery. "I saw you leave the van and I came in here looking for you. I couldn't resist."

"That's it?" I asked, pulling back to get a good look at him. "That's fine, fuck. Do you want to give me a heart attack?" He just wanted to see me. How could I be mad at that?

Ramiro cracked a smile, and I saw those dimples. "That's it?"

"Yes," I said, scowling up at him. "I thought the worst of you right now, Ramiro."

His small smile turned into a little chuckle, and I wondered if he knew the hand on my waist was all I could think about.

He slipped underneath my t-shirt, stroking my bare skin with his thumb while his eyes glinted down at me. He didn't look as grumpy as he did before. A light hearted grin was on his face, and I had a strong feeling it was because his hands was on my skin and I wasn't doing anything to stop it.

I can't stop it.

He knew that I liked it.

"I have to go," he whispered dejectedly, leaning over to kiss my shoulder and I wished he'd do more. "I was already on my way somewhere and I think I'm late now."

There wasn't an ounce of care in his voice.

"That's okay," I muttered, running my hand over his cotton t-shirt.

I couldn't deny that I was disappointed, but Ethan was probably on his way back and I'd have no answer to why a man was in my apartment. It was best to avoid the questions.

Ramiro breathed in deeply, and he couldn't hide his reaction to my hand gliding over his chest. I pulled back before the both of us succumbed to the other.

There was no time. It wasn't the place. If I could've, I'd tell Ramiro there was no rush for him to leave.

"I'm going," he said, his eyes telling me that it was the last thing he wanted to do. "But can I see you again? Soon?"

"You'll come to me?" I asked.

"Yeah," he murmured, nodding his head. "I'll come to you."

"Yes."

I didn't think about the question, or the possibilities it might bring. I was trying to understand Ramiro and the person he was. Why did he walk around with a gun? Why did I want to fuck him right there? Why did I want him to stop being good even when he promised? How did every sliver of restraint vanish the second he looked at me with those green eyes?

I watched him smile at my answer.

"Good," he whispered, his eyes glinting with a certain mischievousness I couldn't pinpoint. "Bye, Nova."

Suddenly feeling as nervous as I did before, I watched Ramiro walk through the door.

"Bye, Miro."

When he closed the door behind him, I felt my chest fall as I took a deep breath in.

What did I agree to? I couldn't imagine that I'd have an easy time staying away from him. He knew where I lived. He knew that I couldn't resist him. He knew that the unfazed façade I put on was one big lie. Ramiro saw right through me and the regret I felt about leaving.

And he liked it.

I'd just proven that to him by saying a simple yes to his request.

Two minutes later, Ethan came back with two milkshakes in either hand. He entered with a stupid grin on his face, holding the milkshakes as if they were trophies in the air.

"What?" he asked, frowning at me.

"Nothing," I said, shaking my head at him. "Nothing at all."

CHAPTER 7

"**I** can't believe he fired you."

"I know," I murmured, glancing up from my computer for the first time in twenty minutes.

Everything hurt and all I did was sit on a hard, wooden chair for two hours. My muscles were stiff. My eyes needed a break. I was hungry. My day had an awful start and as I sat at my desk looking for job openings, I started to despise Paul all over again.

What a fucking inconvenience to my life.

Why is nobody hiring?

Maybe I should take his advice and have my tits out for the next interview. Asshole.

Jade was sprawled over my bed while she texted her long distance boyfriend—giggling every now and then with a certain glint in her eye.

She missed him, and then she didn't. She wanted to leave him, and then she didn't.

It was complicated and I stopped trying to understand their relationship a while ago. I just nodded my head and found her complaints entertaining enough.

She smirked, a cheeky look on her face when she looked up at me. "I can't believe you went and fucked a man you knew for two minutes on that same day."

My mouth dropped. I never should have told her and at the same time, I couldn't not tell her. I had to speak to someone, right? I was going to burst if I didn't.

Ramiro had found his way into our conversation and Jade notoriously lived for the gossip. She didn't know the details—but she knew enough to know that I slept in a stranger's bed after he took me home and tired me out.

Maybe that is too much information.

"Two minutes?" I grinned, grasping at a soft pillow to throw at her. "It was at least five."

I think. Was it two minutes?

He had me in his bed longer than he knew me.

She chuckled, turning over onto her stomach. "Girl, I'm jealous."

Her laugh faded into a solemn sigh.

"What's wrong?" I asked her, dropping the pen I'd been holding. I wasn't using it. I liked having something to hold in my hands while I skimmed the internet.

I glanced over at Jade when she didn't say anything, finding her silence alarming. She always had something to say. Her lower lip was caught between her teeth and I saw the question on her face.

I gestured with my hand, willing her to speak before I threw something harder than a pillow at her.

"Nothing," she muttered, rolling over to her back to stare at the ceiling. "Was it easy?"

"Was what easy?" I asked, scowling at her.

She let out a breath, resting her hands on her stomach. "You know..."

"No, I don't know."

"Jade, what?" I pressed again, frowning at my friend.

She raised her hands exasperatedly, groaning out in frustration before turning to look at me.

"I'm upset, Nova. Dylan is all the way over in Korea and I'm here. Underpaid, overworked and sex-less. I just—why does he have to be so far?" Her forehead dropped onto the mattress, muffling the sound coming from her mouth.

I cracked a smile, but her quick glare had me dropping any humour from my face.

Jade was scary when she needed to be. She was also asking if it was easy to find a man who wanted to take me home. Or maybe she was asking if it was easy to let loose. The answer was yes to both.

Was it easy? Ramiro made it feel easy.

"He's visiting in two months," I murmured, playing with the hem of my skirt. "Isn't he?"

"Sometimes it feels as if I'd be better off single," she said softly. "What's the point of having a boyfriend if I can't touch him? Kiss him? Fuck h—"

"Jade," I interrupted, letting out a small laugh despite the seriousness on her face. "You love Dylan, don't you? Just wait these two months and when he's here, you're going to wish he'd leave you alone."

Considering my track record, I was not the best person to be handing out relationship advice but I did it anyway—for her sake. I couldn't imagine being with someone for longer than a year. The thought of staying with the same person forever scared me. But Jade was different.

She cracked a smile, her face lighting up. "You think so?"

"Yes, of course."

Suddenly, her eyes widened. "What time is it?"

I glanced over at the time on my computer. "Just after seven."

"Fuck," she gasped, rushing off the bed and grabbing all her things. "I'm supposed to be at work at eight. I still need to go home."

Night shift? She wasn't lying when she said that she was overworked. I couldn't remember the last time we had a chance to go out together. The hospital was always packed. Or they were understaffed.

Jade always complained about it and I let her—as always.

She grabbed her handbag, stuffing her belongings inside which included the nail kit she had used on me. I glanced down at the dark red on my fingers, unable to stop myself from imagining the colour against a certain somebody's tanned skin.

I dropped my hand when the images became too vivid. Why's he still in my head? It had been two days since I saw him, and spoke to him.

He had asked if he could see me and just never showed up again.

I didn't think much of it except that I'd been silently hoping he was someone who stuck to their word.

He didn't say when...

I felt Jade kiss the top of my head in a haste, bidding her goodbye with a wave of her hand.

"Love you, bye!" she shouted, stumbling out of my room.

"Love you!" I yelled back, hearing the stifled noise of my front door slamming shut behind her.

When I was certain she was gone, I slumped down in my seat and let out a tired sigh. I was still unbelievably stiff and I rolled my neck, yawning as I decided to call my search off for the night.

Standing up, I shut my laptop and stretched out my tense body. There was no way I had it in me to keep looking and I realised too late it was probably best if I started handing out printed resumes.

I was in the process of tidying up my desk when a knock sounded from my door.

Jade? Did she forget something?

I skimmed over my room, finding nothing that was hers and my brows pinched together as I grabbed my robe. Sliding my arms through the soft and plush material, I started walking to the living room.

"Coming!" I called out when she knocked again, quickly tying my robe and securing it in place.

I grabbed the handle, swinging the door open and coming face to face with a tall person I wasn't expecting. Ramiro. No, that was a lie. I was always expecting him. I didn't know when but I knew he'd show up.

I had, somehow, convinced myself that I wasn't looking forward to it.

I need to stop.

How many times have I said that?

He stood there and the second his eyes landed on me, I watched a small smile spread across his lips. Ramiro always looked good—but in that exact moment, I wondered how it was possible for him to look better than he did before.

Was it the tattoos? The white shirt? Or maybe it was the way he stared down at me and looked ready for a repeat of our night. Did I want that?

"Hey," he breathed, his grin the most contagious smile I've seen in a while.

I stepped aside, welcoming him into the apartment I was only halfway through unpacking. Ethan was right. I do have a lot of shit.

I glanced over Ramiro and stopped on his hands. "Oh my—"

Without thinking, I latched onto his wrists and looked down at his bruised, red and cut knuckles. What the fuck?

"Have you been hitting brick walls?" I asked seriously, but all he did was chuckle down at me with a playful glimmer in his eyes.

I inspected his hands, skimming over the cuts and bruises. Ramiro definitely beat the shit out of someone. It was obvious. I ran my fingertips over a particularly blue area, grimacing at the thought of being at the receiving end of those fists.

I let go of his wrists and craned my neck to look up at him, finding a wholesome smile on his face.

His dimples showed, conveying how childlike his grin was but I gazed down at his hands and failed to believe that they belonged to the same person.

They did.

They definitely did.

"I'm fine, Nova," he said, his eyes staying on my face as if he couldn't look anywhere else. I scoffed, touching a sensitive spot and hearing him hiss through his teeth in pain.

Sure you're fine.

"Okay. Can I help?" I asked, giving him a look and hoping he wasn't as stubborn as he looked.

He wasn't.

"You can do whatever you want."

Oh?

I closed the door behind him and took his hand in mine, leading us to the bathroom. He followed me without a word. His hands looked like they hurt—freshly so. How recent was it? What happened? I bit my tongue to stop myself from spilling out the questions and I blamed my nosy self.

Ramiro saw that and let out a small chuckle, his voice trailing behind me as I led us down the hallway.

I gestured that he sit down on the edge of the tub and he listened.

Why is he so obedient?

I started rummaging through the cabinet and found ointment, alcohol wipes and gauze. He lifted his hands, waiting for me and I let my own smile spread across my face.

I couldn't remember Ramiro being that compliant. I liked it.

He sat there and I hovered over him, ripping open the packaging with my teeth. Ramiro was in my home, but there was nothing nerve-wracking about it. Oddly enough, he made me feel at ease.

Well, he was inside of me.

What was different about him being inside of my apartment instead?

"How badly did these hurt?" I asked, referring to the tattoos on his hands. I was inkless—too scared to commit to something permanent on my skin, but Ramiro was covered. His pain tolerance must have been through the roof.

I held his palm, spraying a saline solution over the open cuts and bruises.

He winced slightly. "A lot."

"Yeah?" I chuckled. "Is that why you have so many?"

Ramiro grinned, shaking his head. All I could think about was kissing him. In my small bathroom, I could feel his warmth—smell the scent clinging onto his skin. He stared up at me and I admired his eyelashes, quickly averting my gaze to the task at hand—his hand.

He looked like he was having the exact same thoughts.

I need to get a grip on myself.

"I appreciate this, Nova," he said, his voice husky and I noticed the slight bouncing of his knee. "I'm sorry for showing up like this but fuck, I couldn't wait. I wanted to see you."

I cleaned his wounds, feeling my heart starting to race in my chest. Why did he always seem to say the words I wanted to hear?

Ramiro stood up, but I didn't let go of him. With the hand that I wasn't tending to, he touched my chin and I was forced to look up at him. Just looking at him was enough. My body went warm and again, I hated how easy I was.

He traced his fingertips over the length of my neck, letting out a sigh that wasn't far from content. "Thank you, amor."

I ran my tongue over my lower lip. "Can I finish up here?"

Before I lead the both of us to my bedroom.

Ramiro's smirk widened as he sat back down. "Of course."

Chapter 8

"**C**an I ask what happened?"

"Yes," was all he said, watching me while I attentively closed a bandage around his hand.

Yes?

That's it?

I let out a small, subtle scoff and secured the gauze in place. It wrapped around his palm and covered his knuckles, protecting the open cuts I covered with ointment. Thank you, Jade.

While I focused on dressing his wounds, his eyes were on me as if he couldn't look away. I didn't want him to. I could barely keep still and concentrate because all I really wanted to do was look at him too.

His tattooed fingers were in my own hand, and his ring was cold against my skin. How could I concentrate?

"Self-defence," he muttered after a beat of silence, his voice soft in my bathroom.

I glanced down at him at him, searching his eyes and finding nothing but the truth. At least, that's the way it looked.

I nodded, turning to wash my hands at the basin. I opened the tap and covered my palm with liquid soap, ignoring the sound of Ramiro getting on his feet. I washed my hands, covering my skin in the soft scented suds and intentionally paying no attention to the feeling of him coming up behind me.

I rinsed my hands, and his own slipped underneath my t-shirt and found my waist. When did my robe become undone?

His hand was warm, but the bandage was rough and I found myself liking the way it felt. Almost too much. I let out a small sigh, only just stopping myself from leaning into him.

His chest was barely against my back, and I wanted him closer without having to ask for it.

I heard him breathe in, and I locked eyes with him through the mirror to find that his were already fixated on me.

He bent down, and I watched his face disappear when he offered me a kiss on the side of my neck. A small, barely there kiss that had my skin warming up at his touch. His dark hair was full—longer than the first time I saw him. I craved to run my hand through it one more time.

"You're so beautiful," he whispered, his breath fanning against my exposed flesh.

Closer.

"Miro," I whispered, holding the edge of the basin as if it were my crutch. I, shamelessly, leaned my head back and felt his chest.

I didn't want to pretend I wanted him gone. I needed to show that he could stay if he wanted to.

I eyed him through the mirror, feeling and seeing his lips graze over my neck. He left fire in his path and chills followed suit, a sensation I still couldn't get accustomed to. It always felt new.

"Did you have a good day, hermosa?" he asked softly, his tone tender.

"No," I answered truthfully, leaning my head to the side and granting him the access he wished for. He smiled slightly and I observed him through the mirror, feeling every part of me enjoy the view.

"Who do I need to kill?" he mumbled, his voice muffled by my skin and my lips parted when he kissed me harder. I chuckled slightly, but he didn't.

"My ex-boss," I joked, nearly letting out a moan when he gave me the gentlest bite on my shoulder. I couldn't take my eyes off him, and the intention on his face.

Why did he almost seem...at peace?

"Yeah?" he breathed. "Still hasn't paid you?"

"No," I whispered. "I don't want to go back there."

"You don't have to," he said, his hand on my waist squeezing me harder. "You're still looking?"

"I have no other choice," I murmured, swallowing when I felt how hard he was through the material of his pants.

He was close enough for me to feel how big he was, and I wanted to turn around and feel him in my hand instead. Or my mouth. His proximity had me throbbing, but the lips on my skin had me wishing the both of us weren't clothed.

"I know, hermosa." I felt the hand on my hips stroke my skin. "I know."

"Did you have a good day?" I asked, my voice soft when he ran his hand from my hip to my chest. My thick gown had me feeling hot. Or it was his touch. Either way, I wanted it off.

"No," he answered. "A terrible fucking day."

"Yeah?" I breathed, turning around in his hold and seeing the frown on his face. He wasn't done kissing my skin. But I wanted more. His hands moved with me, clutching at my waist underneath the cotton t-shirt I wore.

"Yeah," he said, his eyes darting between my own and my lips. "In two days, I've tried four times to come to you. Something got in the way each and every time." Four times? And he continued to try a fifth?

I ran my hand over the back of his neck, pulling him closer and feeling his lips graze against mine. With a relaxed face, his body was anything but. He was tense, his hands curling into my skin and sending the message he didn't say out loud.

His breathing had quickened, and a small sound fell from his lips when I had my hand in his hair. It reminded him of something.

I looked up at him and rested a palm on his chest, already fucking wet for him.

Easy.

"You're here now," I said quietly, his lips hardly touching mine as I spoke.

I could feel his heart beating under my hand, blatantly showing that he wasn't as calm as he was pretending to be. Me neither.

He was there and I wanted him, silently ignoring the fact that one night stands were supposed to be just that. I couldn't care—not when he looked the way he did. All brunette, green eyed and tanned with a look of utter need on his face. It almost hurt to look at him.

"Nova," he breathed with furrowed brows, leaning over to kiss me. I melted into it. He had been kissing everywhere but my mouth and when he did, I couldn't have it ending too soon.

I let out a small moan and he did too, his lips against mine soft and warm and unbelievably familiar.

He was a great kisser. He kissed as if he meant it. All too intense, and impassioned. He took it and I let him have it, giving in to the gentle feel of his mouth and the hands roaming my body.

Ramiro sucked on my lower lip, a muffled groan coming straight from his chest. I couldn't grasp how I was annoyingly attracted to him. It didn't make sense. I pulled back and looked at him, finding my answer on his face and the sound he made when I ran my palm over the front his pants.

The night we had spent together, Ramiro made it all about me. He didn't stop trying to make me feel good. I was put in positions I'd never been in before, and his head was between my thighs making sure I'd enjoy it. He took my pleasure and made it his own.

Tonight, I wanted it to be all about him.

I cupped him in my hand, hearing his sharp intake of breath. His head was slightly tilted upwards, staring down at me with a clenched jaw. He's so hard.

I was barely touching him, but his reaction was quick. He grew in the palm of my hand and I tried not to let my eyes show my shock. More? He breathed through his nose, swallowing when I held him harder and looked down at the way he fit in my hand.

"Miro?" I breathed, finding his eyes again.

"Yes?" he asked, his voice strained.

I leaned closer to him, standing on the tips of my toes when I whispered, "you're going to shower with me."

"Yes," he was quick to say—not a sliver of hesitation in his voice.

I held back my own smirk, unable to harbour any doubts when his eagerness was loud and clear. My hand fell from him, and the sudden lack of contact had Ramiro pushing his lips together. He wanted to protest. He wanted to demand that I touch him again and I saw it in the ticking of his jaw.

His patience is everything.

But how much more did he have?

I started unbuttoning his shirt, intentionally moving at a tedious pace. His chest heaved underneath my fingertips, watching me as I took his shirt off.

I looked at the man in front of me. All bare, and inked. He was stunning to look at.

I breathed in and ran my hand over his smooth chest, sliding over the indents on his stomach. He shuddered underneath my touch, and I smiled when his hands curled into fists. His body was perfect—a hard worker who had the scars to show for it.

I didn't want to stop touching him, but I wanted my clothes off too.

"Nova," his voice was almost a whimper, his brows pulled into a look of desperation.

My hands dropped from him and I started taking my own clothes off. Standing completely naked in front him, I tilted my head to the side when I saw the look in his eye. He wanted me.

His dark gaze ran over my body, stopping on my chest. He'd have me right there if I let him and I needed him to take it. I turned away from him and worked on warming up the shower, leaning over to mess with the taps.

I knew he was looking at me and I felt the chills on my skin. His presence was powerful. His stare was worse.

But his dick was hard, and I wanted him where I could taste him.

Does he know how badly I needed him to feel good?

I stepped underneath the stream, sighing as I felt the warmth envelope me. Ramiro was behind me, and I felt how naked he was when he pushed against my back.

The water ran over the both of us, but nothing could calm the stampede inside my rib cage. I'm not as calm as I thought. His hand rested on my waist, and I leaned back when I felt his wet lips on my shoulder. I throbbed between my thighs, needing to feel him slip inside of me and fuck me against the wall.

I wanted it more than I could say.

But that's not what we were in the shower for.

"Fuck," he muttered, his arm curling over my chest and I felt his palm on my breasts. "I can't keep my hands off you, hermosa."

"I've thought about this for weeks," he breathed, his groan vibrating through me. "When are you going to get out of my head, Nova?"

I turned around, but he didn't let go of me. I didn't want him to. His arms were around me and I wanted it to stay that way. With his chest against mine and a thin layer of water between us, I looked up at him and traced my fingertips over the veins on his forearm.

"Do you want me to?" I asked softly, scowling slightly.

"No," he murmured, meaning it. "No, I don't."

I smiled, kissing the side of his neck. "Good."

"All I want to do is make you feel good," his voice was barely audible, low and deep. His hand lowered over my back, stopping just above my ass and I almost asked him to touch me. I didn't.

I had one thing in my mind—and that was making sure Ramiro could never get me out of his head.

"Not today," I said, littering kisses all over his skin and living off the noises he made. "It's my turn."

"Hermosa," he whispered, tilting his head back and allowing me to kiss the middle of his throat. "I'm—" he swallowed, cutting off whatever he wanted to say and I smirked when I made my way down.

His body was wet, covered in droplets that fell over his skin. I felt my mouth water, all too keen on having him fuck my throat the way he deserved to.

I lowered myself to my knees and looked up at him, loving the way he stared down at me with parted lips and wet hair. Could a man be breath-taking? Ramiro was.

His v-line was deep, joined by a toned abdomen that tensed when I ran my hand over his thigh. The tattoos on his hips were dark, a piece of art I wanted to trace with my tongue. I sunk lower, staring up at him. Fuck, his dick was right there—all hard and ready for me and I held him in my hand.

I felt my nerves skyrocket.

I didn't let that hinder me. No, I couldn't.

"Nova," he said my name, his voice on the verge of shaking. "Fuck, I wish you could see yourself right now."

Is Ramiro oblivious to how hot he was?

I closed my fist around the base of him, feeling his smooth and warm skin. Everything about him was familiar and yet, it felt as if I were seeing him for the first time. That was inside of me?

I swallowed hard, but I was far from hesitant. I wanted it, possibly more than he did.

I gazed up at him one more time, finding his eyes closed and his breathing heavy. He couldn't look at me. That's how badly he was about to lose himself.

My lips closed around the tip of him, watching his reaction and it was everything I needed. His eyes opened, landing on me and I let my tongue run over the length of his dick. Ramiro let out a shaky moan and his eyes fluttered, a look of pure pleasure written all over his face. It was worth it. But I needed more.

Did he?

"Nova," he said shakily, and my eyes roamed over his neck when his head fell back. "You're killing me, pretty girl. Fuck, you're driving me insane."

I stood up and his gaze snapped to mine when I whispered, "Are you going to fuck my mouth, Miro?"

His jaw clenched and I almost faltered underneath his intense, lust-filled gaze. "Yes."

I smirked, returning back to my position. Without a second wasted, I closed my mouth around him and heard his gasp. I didn't wait to wait anymore. I wanted to chase his noises, hear his whimpers and relish in the feeling of his hand on my head.

This time, I didn't pull away as he was expecting me to. I took him deeper, filling my mouth up with him as deep as I could possibly take him. He was big, but I opened wider and felt him in the back of my throat.

My eyes rolled back, but he let out a strangled groan and I couldn't help but moan at the sound of it.

"Oh, fuck," he hissed out, cupping the back of my head but not moving me. I sucked him hard, closing my eyes as I palmed his thighs. It was hard taking all of him. He was so deep I couldn't even breathe through my nose.

His hand stretched out, resting on the wall in front of him and I felt the cool tiles against my back.

I used my hand, stroking him each time I slipped his dick out of my mouth. He grunted and let out a small whimper, eyeing me with furrowed brows and a look of nothing but pleasure.

"Oh, baby," he gasped, stroking the hair from my eyes. "You take all of me. Fuck, that feels good. That feels good, hermosa." That was nothing but motivation.

I had him in my throat and I kept him there for a second longer. He moaned, breathless and wet and hard inside my mouth.

Why didn't I do that sooner?

He was focused on me and never gave me the chance to.

In my shower, I savoured the moment. He was verbal, and I liked it. He was desperate, and I liked it. I ran my tongue over his dick, watching as the arm holding himself flexed.

Ramiro had a terrible day, and I wanted to make it better.

"Fuck," he hissed, throwing his head back and I eyed him from below. "You're a good girl, aren't you?" he breathed out, and I would have grinned if my mouth wasn't busy.

Still, it didn't feel like enough. I wanted Ramiro to fuck my mouth. I wanted him to take all I had to offer. I ran my hand over his side, finding his hand in my own. He knew immediately. He saw it. Ramiro held the back of my head and I kept still.

"Yeah?" he breathed, holding his dick and dragging the tip of him over my already swollen lips.

"Yeah," I whispered, nodding my head.

My hands dropped to my sides and I opened my mouth for him, inviting him in. Ramiro was against my tongue before I could blink.

He fucked my mouth, moving his hips while his hands inter-twined through my hair. The look on his face was priceless. He loved it. I gasped for air when he pulled out. With a grunt and baritone moan from him, Ramiro used my mouth like a toy for him.

I moaned, feeling my throat and lips stretched out from the sheer size of him. His noises were louder, and I knew he was close.

"Wait," he gasped, staring down at me. "Wait, wait. I can't—"

"You can," I encouraged him, my voice muffled around him.

He thrust into me, pleasuring himself and I felt my pussy throb harder. He was into it. Ramiro moaned and I felt the tip of my nose touch his pelvis. My cheeks were hallowed and I sucked him, needing to hear every sound he was capable of giving me. He fucked my throat and with a drawn out moan, Ramiro came.

"Fuck," he grunted. "Hermosa. I'm—"

"I know," I moaned, swallowing every last drop of him and enjoying it. His orgasm came quicker than I thought it would. My jaw was barely tired. Did I do...a great job?

I licked him up, keeping my eyes on him while I did so. I wanted to taste him and I did. He was still trying to catch his breath, holding himself up with his hands against the wall. I stood up and his gaze followed me, his eyelids low and in a drunken haze.

"That was," he whispered, his hand reaching out to me. "Nova, that was—"

I grinned, proud of myself.

Turning around and away from him, I continued my shower while he stood there with his mouth agape.

CHAPTER 9

Ramiro wanted to feed me—but not in that way.

I held back a smirk, watching as the half-naked man fix a plate for me in my kitchen. He wanted to. No, he demanded that I sit down on my ass while I put him to work.

I had mentioned how hungry I was and he couldn't wait to get behind the stove.

He was also visibly shaken.

I had sucked the soul from him and he couldn't have made it more obvious. Did he know I had a lot more to offer than that? I grinned when his eyes met mine, that familiar glint showing all the words he didn't say.

He turned away, shaking his head and I sipped on the drink he had made for me. Ramiro was almost speechless and it made my head swell.

What's wrong with me?

I watched the muscles in his back flex underneath his tattoos, and the sight was hard to stray from. His skin was tanned, covered in ink and a few feet away. It was hard not to continuously touch him.

I ran my tongue over my lip, enjoying the view far too fucking much. It wasn't late, and I didn't know if he had anywhere to be. But even if he left here with nothing but the memory of my eyes looking up at him, I couldn't complain.

He grabbed a plate and started dishing up. It was a pasta—linguine covered in a red sauce that he had made. He was quick, and I was jealous.

It usually took an hour for me to just decide what I wanted to eat, and he had a meal set up in less than thirty minutes.

"Here you go, amor," he said, sliding a plate and fork my way. It looked good. It smelled good. My mouth watered, but Ramiro didn't grab a plate for himself and I gave him a look.

"You're not going to eat?" I asked, scowling at him.

"I'm good," he said casually, grabbing a cloth to wipe the hands he had just washed.

"Ramiro."

"I want to leave enough for later in case you get hungry again," he said, frowning at me as if he couldn't believe I was declining his gesture.

"Please don't fuck with me," I said, sighing. "Sit down."

Eating in front of anyone seemed like a nightmare to me. Eating in front of the person who had taken the time to make it for me seemed unfathomable. I wanted him to enjoy it with me.

His eyes lingered on me, a ghost of a smile trailing on his lips. "Okay, ma'am."

I nodded, waiting while he chose to dish his food in a shallow bowl instead. His preferred dish, I suppose.

He grabbed a fork, seating himself opposite me and I grabbed the fork he had set down for me. I wasn't just hungry. I was starving. He must've been too.

I didn't know where Ramiro came from before me, but his wounds were too fresh and I replaced the wet bandage with a dry, clean one. I didn't want to pry. At the same time, I wanted to know about the self-defence story.

"This looks amazing," I murmured, twirling the pasta around my fork. It truly did. It was even better that all I had to do was be there.

As I sat on the chair, I realised that we were essentially having dinner together. It didn't feel odd. I didn't expect it to. Ramiro was inside of my throat and cooked a meal for me afterwards. If that wasn't the perfect ending to a shitty day, I didn't know what was.

"Yeah?" he asked, smiling from opposite the table. "I hope you like it, hermosa."

I took my first bite, frowning at my plate. Fuck. This is almost better than sex. I took another, and another. It was delicious. It reminded me of an expensive restaurant I had visited a couple of times.

Ramiro can cook.

Could food taste beautifully? It definitely did. I looked over at him, waving my hand and gesturing that he stop admiring me and eat. Ramiro hadn't stopped looking at me as if he wanted to eat me.

"Okay," Ramiro chuckled breathlessly. "I guess you do."

"Of course I do. Can I have you as a personal chef, please?" I joked.

He looked up from his bowl, locking eyes with me and with all the seriousness in the world he said, "Yes."

"Sure," I muttered, rolling my eyes. Ramiro scoffed, his lips pursing as he stopped himself from saying anything else.

I grinned, digging into my food again. I didn't want it to get cold. I finished up, and Ramiro did too. When our plates were completely empty, I realised just how much he had dished up for me. That was a lot.

I ran my hand over my stomach, sighing in pleasure. I couldn't remember the last time I had eaten to the point I was full. I wanted it again.

"Thank you, Miro," I said appreciatively, unable to move. "That was good. Are you available Thursday night?" I asked, and I was joking but Ramiro didn't seem to take it as such.

"Yes," he said. "Do you like steak?"

"I was—"

"Don't care," he interrupted. "Do you like steak, Nova?"

I grinned, and it was against my control. "I do."

"Good," he murmured, not a single trace of humour on his face. He was serious, and I had to hide my smile behind the drink I took a sip from.

Was he just good at everything? The drink tasted like something I'd pay money for too.

"Mashed potatoes?" he asked, his eyes on me while he eagerly awaited my answer.

I bit my lip, smiling because I couldn't tear my gaze from the man before me. "Yes."

"Broccoli?"

"My favourite vegetable."

"Good," he deadpanned, standing and grabbing our empty plates. "It's a date."

A date? I didn't hate the idea. Who the fuck was I kidding? I looked at Ramiro, and a small date with the man who'd seen every part of me seemed like the best thing that's happened in two weeks—besides the event that happened one hour ago.

Was my life boring? Or did Ramiro just have that effect on me?

I breathed in, leaning my head back as I thought about everything I didn't say out loud. Why was he cooking for me? Why was I letting him stay even after the intimacy had passed? Why did I want him to stay a bit longer? Why did it seem as if Ramiro didn't want to leave, too?

"I'll do it," I said, getting up when he started tending to the dirty dishes.

I couldn't allow him to cook and clean. Right? I scowled at him, grabbing the plate from his hand.

He stood there with his lips parted, another confused look on his face. Again, he couldn't believe I turned down his kind gesture. He was a guest. I was supposed to be the one making sure he was enjoying his stay—but it seemed like the other way around with him.

"Nova, I can do it. Just—"

"Ramiro."

"Okay. Fine." He let go of the plate he had been holding onto, surrendering the tedious task of washing up.

I didn't mind it. I'd complain, usually. But I wasn't the one who cooked.

I moved my hand, silently telling him to sit down and relax for a while. He did. He sat down at the kitchen table, facing me. Yet again, he didn't try to look good but he always did. Was it the chain around his neck? His messy hair? The art on his skin? The ring on his finger? Or was it just...everything?

Ramiro smelled good, too. He had used my soap, but it was different on him. How?

"Wow," he suddenly said, his brows pulled into a frown. "You're fucking beautiful, Nova. Can I, please, stand by you? For fucks sake."

"Fine," I murmured, feigning annoyance but I was anything but. I liked having him close to me. It wouldn't last long, and I wanted to take advantage of it in the meantime.

I started washing the plates in soapy water, and Ramiro silently came up behind me.

This time, there was nothing daunting about it.

He closed his arms around my waist and kissed the side of my neck, sighing into my skin. It felt good. Ramiro was touchy. Suddenly, I didn't want the dishes I was cleaning to come to an end.

"When are you going to let me taste you, huh?" he breathed, running his nose over my skin. "It's all I've been thinking about." Me too. I could imagine the feel of his lips and his tongue, stroking all the parts that had me a mess on his bed. I could almost feel it.

I let out a small sigh—a barely noticeable one but the smirk against my neck told me that Ramiro paid attention.

His hand dipped under my big t-shirt. The only thing I wore besides the lace number underneath. He let out the faintest groan, running a flat hand over the curve of my ass and halting at my hip.

I couldn't answer his question. Now? Later? I swallowed, still feeling the soreness in my throat. I hated that I liked the little souvenir he left me with.

"Yeah?" I murmured, closing my eyes.

"Sort of," he whispered, his fingers tracing the hem of my under-wear and he stopped at my lower stomach. "Mierda, this is stunning on you. Is red your favourite colour, hermosa?"

"One of," I mumbled, grabbing another plate. "Is it yours?"

"It is now," he said, his lips moving against my skin as he spoke.

"What else were you thinking about, Miro?" I asked, my voice quiet as I struggled to keep my legs from pushing together. He probably knew about the hard time I was having. His dick was hard against my back, showing me that I wasn't the only one in need of a bed.

Who says we need a bed?

"Everything else," he said, and I noticed his accent was a little stronger than before. "Fuck. Everything else, amor. But the way you taste — I wanted that the most. I still do."

I let out a breath, his words instantly finding its way to the inside of my thighs. I was pulsing, but my heart rate nearly distracted me from the feeling. Nearly.

I finished up the last piece, placing it on the rack but all I could think about was his hands roaming my body.

"Ramiro," I murmured his name, letting the back of my head rest on his chest.

"I know," he said, sliding his hand over the side of my waist.

With one last peck on my cheek, Ramiro stepped away from me. He returned to his chair and with his eyes on mine, he tapped the top of his thigh.

I dried my hands with a cloth, walking over to him without any resistance. There was nothing to think about. Straddling him, I sat on the spot he wanted me at. Ramiro was hard, and I felt him push up between my legs. It strained around his pants, hitting me exactly where I wanted him.

"Are you going to let me stay the night, Nova?" he asked, his gaze darting between my own. His tone wasn't desperate, but he looked at me as if he were hoping I'd say yes.

Could he stay the night?

"Yes," I whispered, my hands on his chest.

He grinned widely, showing those dimples that didn't correlate with the rest of his body. "You su—"

Ramiro was cut off by a loud knock on my front door.

The both of us looked in the direction of the noise, frowning at the rude interruption. Who the fuck? It was almost ten—an unreasonable time for visitors and I glared at the door.

Whoever that was could have fucked off after the third set of knocks.

I waited, and they continued—eventually forcing me off Ramiro's warm body and onto my feet.

"Are you expecting anybody?" Ramiro asked, visibly unhappy with the disturbance.

I shook my head. "I'll just go find out who it is."

Reaching the door, I cussed out loud when I realised I had forgotten that I didn't have a peephole.

"Who is it?" I called out.

"Ethan."

My brother.

Chapter 10

"**E**than."

I let out an annoyed sigh, silently turning to Ramiro. "It's just my brother."

I should've said it's actually my husband and have Ramiro hide in the closet.

Can he go away? Ethan had a bad habit of showing of unannounced. It wasn't regularly, but he popped in whenever he pleased and I didn't find it funny. He had a phone, didn't he?

I looked over at the door, still hearing Ethan knocking his fist against the wood. I almost told him to go away, but I couldn't.

"I don't think I'm ready to meet your family, hermosa," Ramiro said, smirking from where he sat.

"That's disappointing. Here I thought we were making progress," I murmured, cracking a smile, but I was beyond irritated at the interruption.

Ramiro let out a small and deep chuckle, reminding me how stunning his grin was and I really wished Ethan would be quick. I didn't feel for his questions, or the favour he was probably about to ask me. Most of all, I didn't want him to know about the man in my home.

"Nova," Ethan called out, his voice muffled by the only thing between us. "Don't piss me off."

"Miro." I spared him a quick glance. "Please put on a t-shirt."

He was still half naked, casually drinking the tea he had made for himself. Ramiro let out a small, frustrated groan—rolling his eyes when he settled the cup back down on the table.

He wanted to do anything but that.

He stood up, giving me a slight wave of the hand and I watched him walk over to my room. I was quickly distracted by his back and the tattoos and the muscles, until the harsh knocking on my door snapped me out of my thoughts.

Finally opening the door, I came face to face with Ethan. He stood there, irritation plastered all over his features.

"Took you long enough. The fuck is the matter with you?" he asked, scowling at me when he pushed past me and into my apartment. I closed the door behind him, running my hand over my face as I tried to hide how much I didn't want him there.

He was, indirectly, cock-blocking me.

"What's wrong?" I asked, tying my gown.

It didn't seem like there was anything wrong with him. Still, it would have been nice if he told me he was on his way. I glanced down the hall, knowing that Ramiro was just a few feet away and he was about to show up any second.

Perhaps he'd stay there until Ethan leaves.

I doubted it. Ramiro seemed far from the kind to hide away.

Ethan looked over me, frowning. "You're getting ready for bed? Are you seventy?"

"I feel seventy," I said, shrugging at him. Sometimes, I truly did. My gaze drifted from Ethan's face to the hall behind him, watching as Ramiro walked while tugging a t-shirt over his head.

He covered his chest until the fabric covered his stomach, and it was in that moment when Ethan turned to look at him. I didn't see Ethan's face, but I heard his voice.

"Diaz?" he said, his tone hard and stiff and then he turned to me, glaring. "You're kidding me, right?"

His face was hard, almost stoic but he gazed down at me as if I had betrayed him.

"What?" I murmured, confused as I looked from Ethan to Ramiro. "Wait, do you know each other?"

Ramiro didn't seem bothered. No, he was almost amused. He stood there, arms crossed and leaning his shoulder against the wall. Ethan, on the other hand, was giving me the death glare and I felt my heart drop.

Wait, did I fuck Ethan's friend?

I looked at his face. No, there was no way he'd be that upset about a friend.

"Do we know each other?" he repeated, mocking me. "Why the fuck is Ramiro in your house, Nova?" I gave him a look, dropping my arms and feeling the urge to hit him in the face surge through me.

How could he talk to me like that?

He scoffed at me and walked over to Ramiro, who stood unmoving even as Ethan got all in his face.

"Is this some sick joke, Diaz?" he asked Ramiro, standing close to him but Ramiro didn't look like he was intimidated. Far from. "You fucking my sister now?"

Wow.

Ramiro didn't seem amused anymore. He pushed himself off the wall, only growing taller and towering over a shorter Ethan. I'd never seen him that serious before. I stood there in the living room, incredibly confused.

I almost...didn't want to say anything.

I ran my tongue over my lip, ignoring how hot serious Ramiro was and the way his jaw ticked. Now is definitely not the fucking time.

"Ramiro," Ethan snapped. "What are you doing here? Here to fuck my life over, again?"

I wasn't speaking, but that didn't mean I wasn't thinking. Ramiro knew Ethan. Ethan knew Ramiro. They both didn't like each other. Actually, it seemed like a one-sided beef that Ethan was fixated on and Ramiro couldn't care less.

I sighed.

Ethan always interrogated the boyfriends I'd bring home with me. It wasn't new. But I knew, for certain, that it almost had nothing to do with that. Or me, for that matter.

"Ethan," Ramiro murmured, his voice soft but his eyes cold. "Do you want to talk outside?"

"No," Ethan deadpanned. "I want to know why you're in my sisters apartment?"

Ramiro shrugged, nodding to the kitchen. "I cooked her dinner. What are you doing in your sister's apartment?"

"That's none of your business," Ethan snapped through gritted teeth, pointing at the door. "Get the fuck out. Right now, Diaz. I'm not fucking around."

Ramiro didn't say anything, but he looked over at me as if he were awaiting my answer. If I told him to leave, he would. If I told him to stay, he'd do it.

It meant that Ethan could have forgotten about telling him what to do when it wasn't his place to do so.

But what kind of sister would I have been if I forgot about all the times Ethan had saved me from dumbass situations I put myself in? Was Ramiro bad? Is that why he had the gun? I, clearly, didn't know anything.

I let out a breath, annoyed by the amount of testosterone floating around my apartment. Both of them should leave, actually.

"Ethan," I murmured, and his gaze snapped to mine. "What's happening here right now? You barge in here, acting like this for no reason—"

"No reason?" he asked, letting out a humourless chuckle. "You have this—this piece of shit in your apartment and I'm acting like this for no reason?"

"Nova," he said, walking over to me and I felt my blood run cold because it almost seemed as if he wanted to hit me. "Nova, look. Who is this, huh? Who is Ramiro to you, huh? A friend? A lover? Do you know what he is to me? I can't believe I'm having this fucking conversation with you. He's nothing but bad fucking news, Nova. And you won't believe me until he fucks you over, right?"

"Get away from me, right fucking now," I snapped at him, pushing him away. A flare of anger rushed through me. My brother was in my face about something I had absolutely no idea about.

He was yelling me, and I don't even know what I did wrong.

I glanced at Ramiro, finding his eyes already on Ethan. He w as...waiting. For what? My chest heaved, needing Ethan to make himself disappear. He looked down at me—confused.

Why did I push him when he was trying to protect me?

"You," Ethan blurted, reaching out to the back of his pants. "You get out of my sisters apartment. Now."

"Now!" he yelled out, drawing his gun and pointing it directly at Ramiro. "I told you. The next time I see you, I will shoot you. I asked you to leave, Diaz. I asked you. Get out. Or crawl out."

"Ethan!" I gasped. "Are you insane?"

What could Ramiro have possibly done to have Ethan hate him that much?

Ramiro didn't move. He was standing, watching the barrel of Ethan's gun and I watched his eyes flick to mine.

I was in shock. My brother was a nuisance and irritating—but he wasn't violent. He'd never been. He made jokes and wore silly hats but he stood there, pointing a gun at my supposed one night stand with nothing but hatred dripping from him.

He was ready to kill Ramiro.

Why?

"Five years of my life," Ethan snapped through gritted teeth, eventually letting out a dark chuckle. "What? You don't have a gun on you? You losing your touch, boss?"

Five years of what?

"Why would I bring a gun to where your sister lives?" he asked casually, his tone provoking Ethan. "Don't you know how dangerous that is?"

"Did you know? Did you know she's my family?" Ethan asked, his brows furrowed as he waved his gun around.

Ethan was losing his mind. Ramiro didn't even have his hands up.

His gaze met mine. "No."

"And even if I knew she was your sister," he continued, his voice calm as he looked back down at Ethan. "I'd still be here."

"Why?" Ethan pushed, stepping close enough to have the tip of his gun directly at Ramiro's chest. "Why? Anyone in the world. Anyone. And you're here with the only family I have left. You just take and take, don't you? Nova, I have not met a more selfish person than this one you're so desperate to keep, right? Is that why he's cooking you dinner?"

My hands curled at my sides. Keep? He spoke as if Ramiro was a pet.

I barely knew him. Was that true? Probably, but I knew enough to know that if Ramiro had any intention of hurting me, he'd have done the night he took me home.

"You need to stop." I found my voice. "Please. Ramiro has not—"

"Hurt you? Do you want to wait and find out?" Ethan murmured, turning to me but keeping his gun pointed at Ramiro. "Nova. Do you think he's telling you the truth? He didn't know who you were? Do you believe that?"

This is giving me a headache.

"I didn't," Ramiro said, his glare fading into annoyance. "You're loud as fuck, you know that? I didn't know Nova was a Moreno and I've already told you it wouldn't have changed a thing. Now, put that away if you're not going to shoot me. You don't even realise how much you're scaring your sister."

He shook his head, disappointment written all over his face. Even as Ethan's gun stayed on him, Ramiro looked at me as if he was more concerned for me.

This is all so dramatic, for what reason?

So dramatic Ethan had to grab his weapon? He was going to shoot Ramiro on my cream carpet instead of taking it outside?

He was going to be fine with me seeing that shit?

I walked over to my door, grasping onto the handle.

"Nova," Ethan looked at me, his face softening. "I'm sorry. Please, just tell him to leave. Tell him he'll never see you again, and I'll explain why. I'll tell you everything. Just have Ramiro leave. He'll listen to, right? Like the puppy that he is, he'll listen to you."

"Would you?" I asked Ramiro, meeting his gaze.

For a moment, I saw the break in his expression. We had a good evening—a night that I needed and he made me feel the best I've felt in weeks. He looked at me as if he couldn't believe that I was asking him that in the first place—as if our time together meant nothing.

His gaze bored into mine, clenching his jaw as if it were the last thing he wanted to say. "Yes. Yes, I would."

"Ethan," I called, opening the door. "You can leave."

"Me?" he asked, his mouth dropping as he pointed the gun at himself. "You're asking me to leave? Your brother?"

"Yes," I said firmly. "Let me figure this shit out on my own. I'll talk to you tomorrow."

"Nova—"

"Now," I blurted out, my voice louder. "Now, Ethan."

"That's fucked up," he whispered, dropping his gun as he walked over to the door.

When he stared down at me, I felt the chills on my skin. "I really hope you don't regret this, Nova."

And then he was gone, shutting the door behind me loud enough for the sound to echo through my apartment. At the realisation that he was gone, I couldn't help but think to myself; me too.

CHAPTER 11

I slumped against the door and leaned my head back, slowly trying to understand what the fuck just happened.

Nothing made sense.

I hated the feeling of being confused, and that's exactly what Ethan did to me. No explanation. No reasoning. Just guns and ego.

I sighed, feeling Ramiro's hand slip around the back of my neck until I was forced to look up at him. When did he get so close? He was still there. I didn't want him to leave, but I couldn't help but feel as if I was supposed to. I'm supposed to, right?

His gaze was soft, apologetic. "I'm sorry, hermosa. Are you okay?"

"Yes," I reassured, but his concerned stare didn't falter. "I'm good."

His thumb stroked my cheek, his brows furrowed as he glanced over my face. Not only did Ramiro seem concerned, but he looked visibly upset. His intense stare didn't waver. He ran his hand over my jaw and I melted into his touch. Fuck, what's wrong with me?

How was Ethan gone and Ramiro was still there?

I paused, freezing in his grasp. There was no way I just did that. My heart had finally calmed down—the attempted murder in my apartment almost a thing of the past. Almost. No, it happened two minutes ago and I was still shocked.

I just needed to talk to Ethan again—perhaps like civilised human beings this time.

Ramiro stroked his hand over my arm until he latched onto my hand, bringing it up to his knuckles. A kiss was planted on my skin. His mouth was warm, and inviting and soft and I didn't want him to stop. But all I could think of was that there was a reason Ethan hated Ramiro—a reason neither of them wanted me to know about.

A secret I had no business being involved in.

I was wary, and I couldn't help but be.

"Ramiro," I whispered, watching as he laid my palm against his cheek. "It looks like you're saying goodbye." It did. It's probably best if he was.

He was affectionate, but in a way that meant I wouldn't see him for a while and it had me scowling up at him.

This has to be a joke, right?

"I should go," he said, his voice barely audible when his eyes met mine.

"Are you serious? No," I muttered, frowning at him. "I need to know why my brother almost killed you two minutes ago." Am I the only one who thinks this is a big deal?

He let go of me, pursing his lips. The contemplation on his face scared me. He knew why, and he was pondering on whether or not to tell me.

Ramiro was thinking, and I stepped away from him when he didn't say a single word. What if Ethan wasn't over-exaggerating?

If anything, what if his reaction was completely valid and I had the worst human in my apartment?

I stared at Ramiro, unable to read him.

"Nova," he said softly, the sound of my name floating through the empty space between us. "Don't look at me like that."

"Like what?" I asked, feigning obliviousness.

"Like you're trying to figure me out," he said, and the tattooed hand on the side of my neck had me stilling. "Please. I just think it'd be best if you heard it from Ethan. He's the one who knows everything, right?"

It's not something small, or trivial. Ethan had mentioned five years. I tried to wrap my head around it, and the look on Ramiro's face told me to stop thinking.

I paused, letting my tongue run over my lower lip but I didn't say anything.

"I'll talk to Ethan, okay?" he said, and I tried to tell if he meant it or not.

"You think that's a good idea?" I asked, furrowing my brows.

He shrugged, his gaze falling to the side. "I don't know. I can't have that happen around you again, hermosa. Fuck, I really don't want to leave."

What if Ethan came back? What if he came back with an explanation that changed my entire perspective of the man who had me wishing he'd never go?

There was an eerie feeling settling in when I realised that after all that, I'd most likely never see Ramiro again. I nodded at him, watching the conflicted look on his face.

His dark eyes lingered on me, and the hand on my neck fell to his side. He didn't want to leave. He had to. My gaze dropped to the floor and I let out a sigh, feeling my head start to ache as if I'd been sitting in front of a computer for hours.

I should just fuck off to bed.

I was tired of the day. My jaw hurt. I had a full belly. I was showered. Yes, my bed sounded better than anything else—whether Ramiro was next to me or not.

Ramiro lowered his head, bending over to gaze up at me. "Amor."

"What's wrong?" he asked, scowling. "Headache?"

"Yeah," I said, annoyed at the little hindrance. "I'm going to bed."

"Is there anything I can get for you?" he asked, lifting the bottom of my chin with two fingers. "Before I leave?"

"It's already going away," I muttered, smiling at his worried face. It was hard to fault him when he shook his head and walked over to the kitchen, grabbing my bottle of water.

I took it from him, giving him an appreciative grin in return. Drinking the cool water, I felt instantly better. It soothed my dry throat too, and Ramiro smiled at me when I finished.

This is who I'm supposed to be scared of? How?

"Good girl," he said, taking the near empty bottle and closing it. "You want me to stay till you feel better, hermosa?" This is who I was supposed to chase out of my house? I needed to speak with Ethan before I lost my mind.

"I'm okay," I mumbled, meaning it. I thought about how he said he'd stay the night, but that was before Ethan showed up for a reason he didn't even get to say.

Ramiro nodded, still seemingly unconvinced.

"Okay, I'm going," he whispered, stepping closer and I felt his palm on the back of my head. "You know I don't want to, right? I'm not leaving because of your brother. I have somewhere to be and I didn't know until ten minutes ago. Please tell me that you understand."

Why did it mean so much to him? He could have easily said that he'd never see me again. Or that he didn't have time for bullshit that didn't pay him. Instead, he had managed to convince me that if he could stay, he would.

"I understand."

"Okay," he breathed, giving me a deep kiss. I didn't expect it, but I didn't wait to kiss him back. His lips on mine, and I felt him groan—it sounded like a complaint. "Fuck. Okay. Why's it always so hard saying goodbye to you? Okay, I'm going."

I chuckled at him. How many times has he said that? He grinned too, showing his deep dimples and the little glint in his eye when he looked at me. He gave me one last kiss on the back of my hand, and I watched him grab his things afterward.

I wondered what was suddenly urgent. Ramiro didn't say. All I knew was that it had nothing to do with Ethan. I almost scoffed out loud. It might not have anything to do with him directly, but Ramiro wasn't telling me the full truth.

Did I want to know? Yes. Was I going to do anything to find out? Yes. I was two seconds away from dialling Ethan's number and calling him back.

Ramiro was quick to leave, giving me a sharp slap on the ass on his way out.

I grinned, shaking my head at him when he shut the door. I liked Ramiro—possibly a lot more than I was willing to admit out loud but what if I was wrong about him?

What if it was all one big façade? If so, he was a damn good actor. I sighed, deciding to forget about everything for the rest of the night and take myself to bed.

It was two days later when I woke up to a surprise message.

Hi, Nova. I hope this email finds you well. If you're able to, please come into the office today. There is something urgent I'd like to discuss with you.

-Paul

Why did my ex boss want to talk to me?

That was how I ended up at the office. Against my better judgement, I took the drive out of sheer curiosity. Was I getting my job back? I didn't care, at that point.

I wanted to discuss the fucked up payslip he had given me. Or demand that I receive at least another months pay.

Walking in, I spotted Spencer chatting to the newest employee. He was leaning against the water dispenser, a cup in his hand as he flirted with the pretty blonde girl. He didn't see me, and I didn't want him to.

I aimed for Paul's office, and ignored the new secretary on my way in.

"Nova," Paul muttered, his grin unbelievably friendly. "You made it. Please, sit down. How are you?"

I sat down on the leather chair. "This isn't a social call. You said it was urgent."

Paul nodded, his demeanour the opposite of the last time I saw him. It was odd. There was no arrogant smirk, or the nasty look in his eye. He avoided looking at me and I raised a brow at him.

His smile was also uncharacteristically sweet, and it concerned me. Where was the egotistical asshole who fired me?

"Right," he said, sitting down opposite me. "I'm afraid there's nothing to discuss. I actually wanted to give you something, Nova. I hope you accept my offer."

"And that is?" I asked warily, narrowing my eyes at him. "If you mention my tits, Paul. I swear—"

"No! God, no," he rushed out, shaking his hands and head. "I'm really sorry about that, Nova. I didn't mean what I said and I hope you can forgive me—"

"What the fuck?" I whispered under my breath, completely irked out by him. "Can we move on, please?"

"Yes, of course," Paul murmured, sliding a piece of paper my way. "This is what I owe you. And more. A lot more. Just please take it, Nova."

I slowly reached for it.

"Just take it!" he blurted, his eyes wide before his face relaxed into a tight-lipped smile. "Please."

I looked at him as if he had grown another head. Paul never acted that way. He walked around with a rich laugh and his stinking cologne. He eyed everything with malicious intent and lived off the entertainment that came from being a terrible boss.

I stopped moving, watching as Paul stared down at the cheque as if he was desperate that I take it. I did, eventually.

"Wait," I muttered, eyeing the digits written on the check. "This is a year's salary."

"Is it not enough?" he asked, furiously grabbing his chequebook and scribbling with his pen. "Here's another six."

Is he playing with me?

He slid it my way and I took it. Of course. I held both pieces of paper in the air and examined it. There was no way Paul was willingly giving me that. What happened?

I didn't know what to say, but I held onto the papers as if it held my life. In a crazy way, it did.

Paul smiled, clasping his hands together. "I apologise for the way you were fired. It was uncalled for, and highly unprofessional. I trust that we're able to move past this and be friends. If that is okay with you, Miss Moreno."

I stood up and he did, too. "Is this fake, Paul?"

"No," he laughed nervously. "I swear on my life that it's not. Just accept it. We don't have to see each other ever again."

I nodded, still creeped out beyond reasoning. I didn't argue with him. I left his office with a small goodbye, and headed straight to a different bank to cash it out.

Surprisingly, it worked.

I received my money and drove home with my music on full volume. I still didn't understand it, and I didn't bother to. Paul had given me enough money to last a year and I didn't question it. It felt wrong and at the same time, I couldn't give a fuck.

It was thirty minutes later when I walked back into my apartment. Kicking my shoes off, I undid my ponytail and sighed when my scalped relaxed. In the process of washing my hands, a knock sounded from my front door. Wiping my hands, I scowled in the direction of the noise. I hadn't seen, or spoken to Ethan since that day and I wasn't sure if I wanted to.

"Who's it?" I called out, a little uneasy.

"Ramiro," a familiar voice responded.

I opened the door and Ramiro stood there, holding a brown paper bag and a bottle of wine. His smile was soft, and his eyes were softer. It was our date night—one that I thought was off the books considering what happened.

Immediately, my insides warmed up at the way he looked at me. Fuck, I'm not dressed appropriately. But it didn't even look like he cared.

His eyes drifted over me, an all too recognisable look in his eye. "It's Thursday, hermosa. Are you going to let me in or what?"

CHAPTER 12

I didn't know I'd be that attracted to a man cooking for me.

Especially because it seemed as if he was more than happy to do so. Ramiro worked around my kitchen with ease, leaving no mess behind while he demanded that I sit down and just be pretty.

There was no conversation about Ethan. Or the likelihood that I was a bit too trusting. I let myself take it as it was—just for the time being.

Did I feel unsafe with Ramiro? The answer might have been filled with naivety but it was no, I didn't. The completely opposite, ironically.

I watched him dish up for the both of us, unable to take my eyes off him. He looked better than he did two days ago.

He healed quickly, and there was no need for a bandage on his knuckles anymore. The scars were still there and I gazed down at his veined, skilful hands.

How could the same hands that probably left a face unrecognisable handle me with such gentleness? I thought about it. Was there any connection between that and Ethan? No, Ethan's face looked as stupid and untouched as it always did.

"You okay?" he asked, giving me a quick glance.

How many times has he checked up on me just in the hour he'd been here? I liked it. I didn't always like being asked if I'm okay but coming from him, how could I not?

I grinned, nodding my head and he smiled in return.

"Good," he murmured, grabbing both of our filled plates. "I hope you're hungry."

"I've been hungry since this morning," I said, perking up in my seat when he set the steaming plate of food in front of me.

My mouth watered, and I stopped myself from reaching for the knife and fork. Ramiro gave me a look, frowning at me.

"You didn't eat the whole day?" he asked, sitting down in front of me and I shook my head. "Okay. Eat, hermosa. Don't wait for me. You want wine?"

He was kind, and he was also...not. I didn't think about it for too long or I'd hurt myself.

"Water is fine. Thank you," I responded, reaching to grab the cutlery Ramiro offered. "I feel underdressed."

I did. He was handsome, and I was in the clothes I changed into after visiting Paul: Oh, that reminds me. I gazed from my plate to Ramiro, trying not to let the question show on my face.

No, he didn't. Right?

Quickly forgetting about it, I soaked in the way he looked. His white shirt had been rolled up to his elbows since he started cooking. No tie.

The silver watch on his tattooed wrist looked good on him and I tried not to stare too long. It was hard not to but I wasn't the only one struggling to keep my eyes off the other.

Every chance he got, Ramiro would look at me with those dark green eyes. I'd be reminded of him inside of me—staring down with a half-lidded gaze because it'd be our third time fucking.

Fuck.

I almost sighed. I missed it. I wanted it. Why did I crave it?

"You're in your home," he told me, grinning at me from across my small table. "I don't think you should be dressed anyway, amor."

"Eating naked?" I chuckled, cutting into my perfect steak. "That's wild."

Despite the calm atmosphere, I kept expecting Ethan to pop out from around a corner with a gun and more demands. Did he traumatise me?

Ramiro's car was outside—blatantly out of place and Ethan could show up any second. Fucker. He had ruined the comfort I felt in my own apartment and I almost told Ramiro to take me back to his house instead.

The music was calm, low and far in the background. It helped, and I told myself that Ethan hadn't made an appearance in two days.

Why would he come right in that moment?

Plus, the lock on my door did wonders.

I took the first bite of my food and it made me forget. My eyes almost rolled back. I looked at him, trying not to push my plate aside and sit myself down on his lap.

I was in awe. It tasted good. He tasted better. I grinned at him, incapable of speaking because I was already on my second bite. Ramiro hadn't even touched his food.

"Yeah?" he murmured, giving me a dimpled smile. "Wow, you look so beautiful."

"You're going to make me choke," I whispered, letting out a small chuckle.

"I know," he said softly.

"Eat," I blurted out, rolling my eyes at him.

"I want to."

"Your food, Miro," I said, shaking my head at him and he scoffed a small laugh, finally paying attention to the food in front of him.

He ran his tongue over his lower lip, and my gaze dropped down to it for a second. Shaking away all the dirty fucking thoughts, I busied myself with the meal he made for us.

It'd been three weeks since I met him, and three weeks since I had an orgasm that felt like one.

Why am I thinking about this in front of the steak? Shut the hell up, I told myself.

"Can I ask you something?" I asked Ramiro, not looking at him.

"Yes," he muttered, no hesitation on his part.

I paused, lifting my gaze to his own. "What did you do to Paul?"

Ramiro hand stilled mid-air, his fingers curled around his glass of water before he settled it back down.

"Who's Paul?" he asked, frowning at me.

My face dropped into a look of boredom, wondering if he knew that he was only a good liar when he tried.

"Miro," I said his name, but it was far from threatening. "Really?"

He shrugged, a seemingly confused look on his face. "I don't know what you're talking about, hermosa."

"Ramiro," I said again, narrowing my eyes at him.

"Nova," he said, a small smirk on his lips.

I took a deep breath in. "You're not going to tell me? Fine. I don't want to know anyway. But thank you."

He nodded—the same soft smile spreading across his face. "You're welcome, amor."

"So you know what I'm talking about," I murmured, eyeing him. Of course he did. His smile and the look on his face said it all.

It also said that I didn't need to ask him any questions and I was loaded with questions. Did he talk to him? Threaten him?

"I do." He continued eating. "Did he give you enough?"

"More than enough."

"Good," he said.

I couldn't stop my stupid smile when I shook my head at him. I would have paid to see the conversation that happened between the two of them. Was it even a conversation?

I continued eating, savouring the moment while it lasted.

The questions were on the tip of my tongue and with one look from Ramiro, I kept my mouth shut. He was hard to understand and at the same time, he was not.

I glanced over his face while he drank his water, trying to conceal the fact that I'd been trying to read him. Ramiro didn't want me to know what he did. He was sweet to me, and he wasn't planning on letting me know that there were times he wasn't.

I still had no idea what he did for a living.

Not knowing only mattered when I thought I would only see him for one night but he was there—in my apartment and I didn't know what paid him.

"Keep looking at me like that and I'll fuck you over this table, hermosa," he muttered, cutting into his food and I felt my eyes widen the tiniest bit.

He wasn't looking at me.

I cleared my throat, shifting in my seat when I realised that that was exactly what I needed. I could go months without it but a taste of what he had to offer and I was a whore for more.

"Do you want that?" he asked, locking eyes with me—dead serious.

"Let's finish up here," I muttered, trying my best not to say yes. "I don't know what you do for work, Ramiro,"

It was clear I was changing the subject. I wanted it. I needed it. I didn't know if I had the ability to say no to him.

Why do I need to say no?

He smirked at me, realising that I wasn't as casual as I was pretending to be.

"You never asked," he murmured, his intense gaze following my own.

I didn't say anything. He was right. I never bothered to ask, but it was becoming important. Wasn't it?

He let out a breath, running his hand over his face. "I do too much, amor."

"That's vague," I said under my breath. "Like what?"

"I own the casino we met at," he said, starting to list off things. "I have a dealership that sells fancy fucking cars and I hate it. I used to be a teacher at a preschool—"

"Wait. Wait," I stammered, holding my hand out. "You own the casino? You used to be a teacher? What—" I was not expecting that.

My brows pinched into a frown, finding it incredibly hard to believe him but he wasn't lying.

Is that why the security let him in even though he was carrying?

"I'm not even half way done," he said, chuckling at me. "Do you want to know more?"

"Can we rewind, please?" I said, grinning at his amused face.

He waved his hand, gesturing for me to keep talking and I did—unable to stop myself.

"How did you go from being a teacher to owning businesses?" I asked, the curiosity eating at me. It was impossible, right? Or was I just unaware of ways to make money?

"That's the part I'm leaving out, amor," he whispered, crossing his arms over the table.

The missing gap is what I needed to know the most. I wanted to know how he went from teaching little kids to own multiple companies. He was what? Twenty seven?

It didn't make sense.

But it was always interesting that he used to be an educator. I never would have guessed.

Did the tattoos come before or after?

"Yeah?" I murmured, cocking a brow at him. "Tell me if you're part of a gang, Ramiro."

"I'm not," he laughed, showing his childlike dimpled smile. "Don't worry."

Where the fuck did Ethan fit in?

"Do you promise?" I asked sceptically. The last thing I wanted was being associated with something potentially life threatening.

He was hot, and fucked me good—but that didn't mean I wanted to be cautious around him all the time.

"Yes, I promise," he said, nodding his head. "Did you think I'm the mafia, hermosa?"

Yes.

I grinned, shrugging. "I didn't know what to think, Miro."

"I'm not, I swear," he said, reassuring me when he raised the both of his hands.

"Okay," I mumbled, believing him. "How long were you a teacher for?"

"A year," he answered. "A long time ago."

"The moms must have loved you," I muttered inaudibly, toying with the rim of my glass.

If Ramiro was my kids teacher—I probably wouldn't know how to act. He grinned, obviously hearing me and I narrowed my eyes at him. Oh, he liked that shit.

His smile vanished and he cleared his throat, focusing on his near-done food.

I was done. I was just sitting there listening to him, feeling an unfamiliar surge of jealousy rushing through me. It was no secret that Ramiro was the most attractive person I'd ever seen and I couldn't help but think; am I the only one he's fucking?

Wait, were we fucking? It'd been a while.

"Oh, yeah?" I asked, leaning back in my seat. "Do you want me to kick you out of my house, Ramiro?" I was just joking. Kind of.

I smiled at him when he let out a small laugh. It wasn't a serious conversation and he didn't take it as one.

"You know I'd just take you with me, right?" he muttered, but his eyes didn't convey the joke.

He wasn't lying. I kept quiet, not trusting myself to say anything comprehensible. I'd let him take me with him—as stupid as it sounded.

"If I kick you out, you'd drag me with you?" I asked, smirking at him.

His shoulder lifted with a small shrug. "Of course."

I hid my smile when I took a sip of my water.

"Thank you for the food, Ramiro," I murmured appreciatively. "I loved it."

He didn't say anything. He was looking at me—his scrutinising gaze fixated on my face and I felt my cheeks warm up.

Am I fucking blushing?

There was a certain look in his eye. One that I haven't seen before. His face was serious. And his smile wasn't there. He rested his arms over the table, absentmindedly fiddling with his fingers and I started to feel the weight of his stare.

He looked as if he wanted to fulfil his wish of having me bent over that very table.

"Am I the only one you're seeing, Nova?" he asked softly, the intensity of his gaze having me shift in my seat.

"Yes." My answer came with no hesitation.

"Good," he said, his voice gentle but his eyes couldn't conceal how badly he wanted my answer to be yes. "Is it going to stay that way?"

"Yes."

"Give me your hand," he said, and I did so immediately. He caught my fingertips, bringing my knuckles up to his lips. "You'll tell me if someone tries to fuck with you, hermosa?"

"Yes."

"Good girl," he breathed, and I felt him place his lips on the centre of my palm. "Keep that in mind the next time you need me to take care of something, okay?"

I swallowed, keeping my eyes on him. He wasn't fucking around. I told him about Paul—not thinking anything of it—and a few days later I received a cheque big enough to carry me through the next year. Ramiro wasn't lying, and I felt my heart race at the thought.

"I will," I breathed out.

"I know you will," he said, smiling when he settled my hand back down on the table. "Dessert?"

"That's be nice," I muttered, watching him collect our plates.

You'll tell me if someone tries to fuck with you.

The heaviness of his words had sunk in and as I observed him cleaning up the table, I couldn't shake the feeling that Ramiro had no limits to his request.

Anything, he said.

I stood up, needing to help him and I grabbed the last of the dishes we had used. He grinned down at me, giving me a quick and chaste kiss on my forehead. It was in that moment when I realised that Ramiro meant every single fucking word he had said to me.

And I couldn't help but love it.

CHAPTER 13

"**H**ow tall are you?"

"193cm."

"Oh," I muttered, finishing the last of my dessert.

Tall.

"And you?"

"I have no idea. I haven't checked since high school."

Even in my tallest pair of heels, Ramiro was still taller. It was intimidating, but how could I be intimidated by a man who furrowed his brows and stared down at me with a yearning I'd never seen before?

It was impossible to.

"Mm," he murmured, sliding his hand over my shoulder. "I'd say you're about 170 to 173. That's just my guess." Probably accurate, too.

I glanced over at Ramiro, already finding his eyes on me. We'd been sitting on my sofa—having a conversation about everything.

Well, not everything.

There were things he left out and I did too. He didn't need to know absolutely everything about me, right?

I listened to his deep, accented voice and nearly fell asleep to it. He spoke softly and calmly and I found it hard to stop myself from dosing off while he talked about his home country.

Spain.

He moved away nine years ago, but the accent lingered and I suddenly had the urge to dig out my forgotten Spanish textbook from school. There was a lot I learned about him.

Unbelievably, the university he attended was the same one I dropped out of. What were the fucking chances?

I leaned over, setting my dessert bowl on the glass table in the middle of my living room. Falling back, I was welcomed into Ramiro's hold when he draped an arm over my shoulder. I didn't mind it. No, not at all. I wished he had done it sooner.

Giving him a soft smile, I reminded myself that his phone might ring anytime soon to save me the disappointment.

He has a busy life.

Was I wasting my time with Ramiro? Was there even such a thing as time wasted?

"Is Ethan the only sibling you have?" he asked, his fingertips playing with the hair over my shoulder.

The sound of my brothers name almost sent me into fight mode. He'd been calling me for the past two hours. Ramiro didn't know. I had my phone in my room—on silent. I had sent a text telling him I'm out for the day and I'll talk later.

He was still calling.

Look at you. Blowing your brother off for Ramiro.

What have I turned into?

"Yeah," I said, fiddling with his fingers and trying to ignore the terrible ache between my thighs. "Do you have siblings?"

"A brother," he said. "He's in the first year of college."

"What's his name?" I asked, mindlessly stroking his hands and ignoring how fucking hard he was next to me. The sides of our thighs were touching. I had changed, and showered while Ramiro ordered my favourite dessert.

It was late, and the place had closed already but he had managed to get the cake I wanted with one phone call.

How?

My tongue traced over my bottom lip, tasting the cherry balm I had used. My legs were bare, and Ramiro's eyes stayed on my skin for a moment too long with a longing I had no problem reciprocating.

The only thing on my body was a t-shirt I usually slept in, and a pair of cotton underwear that I didn't always wear. I liked being free in my home, but I couldn't do that when I had a guest over.

He definitely wouldn't mind.

"Camilo."

"Nice," I muttered, sighing when his warm hand touched my skin. Cuddling into his hold, I felt his muscles underneath his shirt. I didn't want our night to end.

Ramiro brought a certain tranquillity with him that didn't make sense. I was supposed to hate him. I was supposed to be upset that he had my brother hating him. I couldn't. It was difficult to. And honestly, I didn't know if I wanted to hate him.

Hating him meant not having him, and that was the last thing I wanted.

I looked over at Ramiro, watching him heave out a sigh and then rest his head on top of mine.

For now, its fuck Ethan. For now.

"Come here, baby," he breathed, pulling his arm back and I sat up when he did.

Ramiro patted his thigh, and I took my place without another thought. I held his shoulders and straddled him, dropping onto the spot that had his eyes fluttering for a second.

I was in need of a fucking—specifically from the man underneath me and he didn't know how badly I wanted him. Did he? From the way he nestled between my thighs—hard and big—he must have felt the same way.

I slid my hand over his chest, almost letting out a moan because I had missed the feeling of him underneath my fingertips.

"Do you know how beautiful you are?" he whispered, gliding his hand over my ass and memories followed his path. "You're the most beautiful woman I've ever seen, Nova."

"Yeah?" I whispered, feeling his big hands give me a squeeze on my ass.

He was touching my skin, and tracing the hem of my underwear. Ramiro let out a soft moan when he cupped me, and heart beat raced underneath my palm.

He swallowed, licking his lips when he nodded. "Yeah."

"I'm not a jealous person," he whispered, his gaze flickering between my own. "But the thought of you being on top of someone else like this drives me fucking crazy, hermosa."

The thought of someone sitting on my spot drove me insane too. I didn't say it out loud. There were times I felt bold enough to but in that moment, all I wanted to do was listen to him.

"Sounds like jealousy to me," I murmured, smiling when a certain look flickered across his face. Why was he thinking about that?

"I know," Ramiro muttered, unapologetically. "Is that fucked up?"

"No," I reassured, sliding my hand over the back of his neck. "It's not."

"Can you kiss me, Nova?" he breathed, his eyes roaming over my face. "Please."

I let my forehead touch his, barely grazing my lips over his own. So soft. So warm. He had a beautiful mouth, and I traced my fingertips over his cheek while I admired him.

His breathing became unsteady, and I stopped my smirk when his jaw ticked. Ramiro was too patient for his own good.

His gaze was soft—an expression I could stare at until the moment he left. He didn't move. He sat there with his hands on my hips, waiting for me to kiss him and I did.

My lips met his, and I felt his fingers hold me a little bit harder. I kissed him deeper, holding the back of his head while I intertwined my fingers through his hair. His response was a moan, and I felt him part his lips for more.

The best part of his kisses were the hands that couldn't leave me. Or it was the eagerness behind his lips moving against mine. The pleasure of it rushed through me, and I tried to make sense of how a kiss could have me cumming right on top of him.

I grinned against him, kissing him through my smile and a small groan came from the back of his throat.

It felt good to be kissed, and Ramiro was a kisser.

His tongue touched mine, our breath becoming one and I felt myself sink into him. He was suffering underneath me. His dick was hard, pressed against the fabric of my underwear and I moved my hips to grind into him.

"Fuck," he breathed, kissing me through his words. "I can kiss you all day, amor."

He sucked on my lower lip, and gave me a gentle bite. The noise I made was small, but Ramiro lips pulled up at the sound of it.

"Do you like it when I kiss you, hermosa?" he whispered, cupping my cheek and I felt his thumb on my lip.

"Yes," my voice was breathless. He pulled away just to look at me for a second.

With a hand on my cheek, I saw the undeniable lust and desperation on his face. When he leaned forward, I closed my eyes again when his mouth enveloped mine again.

He had my heart racing, and he had my pussy fucking soaked on top of him. Then he closed his bruised, tattooed hand around the front of my throat and it was over.

I wanted to fuck him right there—on that couch and in that position.

He tightened his hold, forcing my moans to escape and he took advantage of my open mouth.

I needed him.

"You're so fucking perfect," he whispered, giving me harsh slap on my bare ass. "You kiss me like this and it makes me want to do anything for you."

"Careful with your words, Ramiro," I murmured. "I might just take you to heart."

"Why wouldn't you?" he whispered, sliding his tongue along mine. "You should know by now that I mean it."

"Do you?" I asked, leaning back to stare at him.

My hands were on his shoulders. My chest heaved as I struggled to catch my breath. Ramiro looked back at me with a look that could only be described as need. He wanted me, and he was going to have me the way he wished to.

His hand disappeared underneath my t-shirt, grasping onto the flesh of my ass before giving me a harsh, stinging slap. I gasped, enjoying the sensation far too much to be reasonable.

"Yes, I do," he blurted, forcing eye-contact when his hand held my cheeks. "Believe me when I say that, Nova. I'd do anything you say when you look at me like this—sit on top of me like this. You're fucking soaked and I'd do anything to taste you right now."

I opened my mouth to speak—to tell him that he could have me. Ramiro stood up with me, cutting my words right off and I felt my back land over the sofa. He was on top of me instantly, burying his face in my neck while he kissed my skin.

His hands roamed my body, gliding over my waist until he reached the hem of my underwear.

He started pulling it over my legs.

A knock from my door had the both of us stilling, and I felt my heart drop in my chest.

Ramiro's gaze found mine. "Did you invite anyone over?"

"No," I said, ignoring the uncomfortable feeling between my thighs.

Please don't be Ethan. Please don't be fucking Ethan.

Ramiro didn't move. He stared at me, waiting to see what I'd do. I didn't want him to get off me, but the person knocking was ruining our fucking moment. I was irritated, and I glared at the door when the harsh knocking got louder.

Can everybody just leave us alone?

We really should've gone to his place.

"You want me to get off you, Nova?"

"Miro," I whispered, my gaze softening.

He let out a sharp breath and ran his tongue over his teeth when he pushed himself off me. We both couldn't stand the interruption. Ramiro sat back down, annoyance written all over his face while I fixed my hair.

He sat with his elbows on his knees, and his hands clasped together while he watched me.

I pushed myself up and walked over to the door. Thankfully, my landlord had a peephole installed for me and I peeked through it. Frowning when I saw who it was, I unlocked the door.

Spencer.

What could he have possibly wanted?

"Nova," he grinned when he saw me, quickly opening his arms for a hug.

It came without warning. His arms closed around my waist, and he lifted me off my feet.

Oh my God.

My jaw dropped, completely shocked by his hug and I tapped his shoulder to let him know he needed to stop.

"Spencer, what the fuck?" I muttered, wiping away the creases on my shirt when he settled me back down on my feet. "How do you know where I live?"

"I have my ways," he said cheerily, his grin all too charming. "I wanted to see you—oh."

His steps faltered, and his smile fell from his face when he saw Ramiro.

"Okay," Spencer muttered, holding his hands. "Fuck, I'm sorry, bro. I didn't know you had someone over, Nova."

He looked at me and for the first time since I've known him, Spencer was visibly uncomfortable. Ramiro looked over me, and I felt the intensity of his gaze flow right through me. He stayed seated, eyeing Spencer with a look that could kill and I was nervous that he actually would.

"Okay, I'm going—" Spencer said, turning to me. "Look. I thought you'd want to have that coffee date."

Can he stop?

"I never said it was a date, Spencer," I said, scowling at him. "Can you leave?"

"Yeah, sure, no problem," he muttered. "Again, I'm sorry, bro. Nova and I are just friends, right?"

My eyes widened at him, realising he wasn't making it better. "Go."

"Okay. Okay," he said, waving before leaving and closing the door behind him.

Ramiro didn't say a single fucking word to Spencer, but he had him shaking in his boots. It was almost funny, but Ramiro wasn't laughing. On the contrary. I looked over him, expecting to find that he was still seated but he wasn't.

He walked over to me, and the look on his face told me he was not happy.

Fuck.

CHAPTER 14

"**Y**ou said his name was Spencer?" I asked, eyeing the door he had just closed.

"Why?" she asked, giving me a look that said she absolutely knew why.

I couldn't figure out what I wanted to do with myself. Walking after the man who had wrapped his arms around Nova to lift her off her feet and spin her around was one of the many things I had in mind. Am I fucking insane?

I lifted my hand, holding her underneath her ear and I felt her hands on my chest.

She made it hard for me—hard to think—hard to be rational. I downplayed a lot of things in my life, but hoping that I was the only one who Nova was seeing was not one of them.

She didn't know how I felt.

It was probably way too soon.

She'd run if I told her that the very thought of anyone else touching her had me way too trigger happy. I almost scoffed. It was just a hug. No, it was his body pressed against hers and the shocked look on her face that clearly said it was the last thing she was expecting. Or wanted.

What are we doing?

"Amor," I murmured, staring at her pretty face. "I'm not going to do anything."

It wasn't a lie.

Encouraging Paul to pay her was already treading into dangerous waters. Imagine if I had to find Spencer and teach him to keep his hands to himself by ripping it off his arms.

It would chase her away. Right?

I licked my lips, stopping myself from kissing her. She was painfully beautiful. A walking novelty. Nova had me in the palm of her hand the second we left that casino, and she was entirely too unaware of it.

"Hermosa," I whispered, scowling down at her when I pulled her closer.

I needed her.

She stopped, staring down at the floor and when her eyes met mine again, I wasn't expecting the mischievous smirk on her lips.

It shouldn't have pissed me off the way it did. Smiling? I should have fucked it off her face right then.

I narrowed my eyes at her, wondering about the things running through her head.

Nova sighed, cocking her head to the side. "I thought you said you don't get jealous, Miro."

Miro. I want to offer her the world when she calls me that.

"I do," I forced out, grasping onto her hand when she tried to walk. "And you know I do."

I touched her face softly, enjoying the sight beneath my hand. I didn't want to stop touching her. I stroked her dark hair away from her face, desperate for a better view.

I couldn't stop thinking about her even while I was with her.

Her eyes stared back, all fiery and laced with defiance. Any other day and I'd have fallen on my knees at the look. I was too caught up on hoping that she wasn't about to do what I thought she was.

She pulled back from me, turning away. "And you know you have no reason to."

And she did.

"Nova," I said, my voice low as I caught her hand once again. "No reason to? Please explain what you mean by that."

I know what she means. I wanted to hear her say it. I wanted her to say that she wasn't mine. Or that I wasn't hers. I had no reason to be jealous. I had no reason to feel as I were the only one who could touch her, kiss her or spoil her with her favourite fucking things.

I looked down at her with my heart racing out of my chest. I wanted to be the one doing that to her—for her. Did Spencer know I'd kill him? Did her curly haired rat of a brother know that he couldn't keep me away from her?

"It means—" she said, sucking in a breath and then she gazed back at me. "It means that you have no reason to be jealous of anybody when you're all I want."

I stepped back, staring down at her.

Did she mean that? Her eyes fell back to the floor and I bent down to look up at her face. Nova had a certain hold on me—one that I couldn't understand. I was hoping she meant it.

Her long hair fell over the sides of her face, and I let my fingertips sweep it away from her cheeks. Stunning. I swallowed, forcing myself not to show the need on my face.

How could I feel like this? Was it that one night, or was it the two weeks afterwards when I couldn't get her out of my head?

"Amor," I whispered, catching her attention. "Stop looking away from me."

"Ramiro," she murmured, glancing over at my vibrating phone on the table. "You're leaving now, right?

"No, I'm not," I said, scowling at her when I straightened up. Did she think I would just up and leave? No, I wanted to stay the night with her.

If she lets me.

I wanted to wake up next to her—an act I'd been dreaming of since that morning she left. It was an odd feeling. It was a feeling that consumed me and had me feeling like a man obsessed with her. I didn't care. I wanted her closer and I pulled her, enjoying the way her chest touched mine.

"Your phone," she said, frowning.

"Ignore it," I deadpanned, meaning it. Whoever it was could have wait. I needed to show Nova that my priorities lied within making her believe me when I said she was all I wanted.

"But—"

"Hermosa," I said, grasping onto her chin and making her look up at me. "I said ignore it."

She opened her mouth to speak, but I held her cheeks with one hand. "Say something about that phone one more fucking time." Please do.

Her breath shuddered, showing that she enjoyed my hand on her a lot more than her face was letting on.

Nova had her legs together, and I trailed my gaze over her t-shirt covered body while her eyes bored into my face.

My fingers stayed on her cheeks while I glanced down her legs, silently imagining all the things I'd do to her—for her. How fucked up was it that I craved to be used by her? To hear her say that I couldn't stop until she said so?

Say the word and I'll fall to my knees.

I let go of her, tilting my head to the side as I watched her swallow.

When she stepped up to me and rested her hands on my chest, I ran my tongue over my bottom lip. It was hard to keep my hands to myself, and it was even harder to stop myself from demanding that she touch me too. She stroked my shirt, and I felt my dick harden more.

Nova stood up on the tips her toes and I leaned lower, letting her whisper in my ear. "Answer the phone, Ramiro."

Okay.

I nodded at her, stepping back and heading to the vibrating face down phone on her coffee table.

She watched me with cautious eyes, almost shocked that I did what she asked. But I wasn't. I reached for it, declining the call without looking at the name and I switched it off. Not today.

Turning back to her, her eyes widened when she realised that I had done the exact opposite of what she asked. I didn't care. I walked back to her, and she took an apprehensive step back.

"Miro," she whispered. Oh, now I'm Miro again?

I stared down at the perfect girl in front of me, struggling to keep my hands at my sides. What was she trying? Did she want to rile me up? Tell her that she was important? Did she want me gone?

"Are you done?" I asked, angling my head.

I almost smirked at the look of her. No, she didn't want me gone. Her gaze didn't lie. She wanted me to show her how badly I wanted her and I had no problem doing so. Nova still had her legs clamped together—her hair loose and her eyes fixated on me.

I'd eat her right here.

"Yes," she murmured, blowing out a breath. "I'm done—"

"Good girl." I bent down and wrapped my arms around her thighs, flinging her over my shoulder and ignoring her surprised gasp.

She needed to stop playing with me.

I slapped her on the ass, hearing her let out a shocked moan at the slight sting. Walking over to her room, I made a small promise to myself.

By the end of the night, she would know that I was hers—even if she was far from being mine.

I'll get there.

I ran my palm over her ass, feeling how warm she was and her smooth skin. My patience was wearing thin. I was a mess on the inside. My dick had been hard since I stepped foot in her fucking apartment and her little stunt was my last straw.

Answer the phone? What did she think this was?

I stepped through the entrance of her room's door, needing to give her an orgasm or two.

"Fuck," she gasped out when I threw her down in the middle of her bed. "Wait—"

She was cut off by my hands around both of her ankles, quickly pulling her to the edge with a scowl on my face. I peered down at her underwear, keeping her legs apart to look at her covered pussy and the small amount of ass I could see from the front.

I breathed in, feeling an insane amount of need surge through me. Letting go of her, I reached for her hand and pulled her into a sitting position.

Nova was compliant—easily so.

Despite the small glare, she spread her knees and I touched the inside of her thigh. Soft.

She stared up at me, dragging her tongue over her lower lip when I bent over. I became eye-level with her, and my hand on her thigh traced a bit higher.

I ran the tip of my finger over her underwear, feeling how wet she was through the material. My mouth watered for her. My dick ached for her. I felt my eyes flutter close. It'd been way too long.

"Tell me, hermosa," I breathed, letting my lips barely touch her own. "What did you miss more? My dick inside of you, or my tongue?" Because I'd do whatever you say I should.

I stared at her straight in the eye, unrelenting even when her beautiful self started shying away. I used two fingers to turn her gaze back to mine, hating when she looked away from me.

Nova swallowed, and her answer wasn't verbal.

I watched her carefully, feeling the blood rushing through my veins at the thought of having her either fucking way. She glanced down, and I didn't look away from her when she cupped my dick in the palm of her hand.

My lips parted and when her gaze flicked back to mine, I almost lost myself.

"This," she whispered, giving me a squeeze over my pants.

"Yeah?" I murmured and my lips never left hers when I whispered, "It's all yours, baby. Lie back."

Nova let out a small breath and slowly fell onto her soft white sheets, keeping her legs hanging over the edge of the bed.

I took a second to admire her.

Her t-shirt had hiked up to her ribs, showing her stomach and it was a pleasure to look at her. I only stared for a moment.

Nova's breathing was unsteady, but I was worse and there was no hiding it. Deciding that I had enough fucking around, I hooked my fingers underneath the hem of her underwear and tugged it over her legs.

Fuck.

I'm addicted all over again.

I clenched my jaw, glancing over her soaked pussy. She's gorgeous.

"Miro," she breathed out, and I caught her gaze once again.

"You want me, amor?" I asked, leaning over to plant my hands on either side of her face. She started squirming underneath me, her impatience and desperation flowing off of her.

Nova let out a small grunt, sliding her hands over her smooth sheets and I did nothing but wait for her to say the words.

"More than anything," she murmured, swallowing away the nerves she didn't show.

I smiled at her, leaning down to give her quickest peck on her jaw. More than anything. Could words bring pleasure? Because hers did. I straightened up again, standing over her while I undid the buckle on my belt.

I loosened my button, and dragged my zipper down. I didn't take my pants off yet. I went to my shirt next and undid the buttons—all while she watched with that lust-filled look of hers and her elbows propped up on the bed.

She looked at me as if she liked what she saw, and it made my head fucking swell.

I reached the last button, and Nova's eyes were zeroed in on my abdomen.

She likes that.

I got rid of my shirt, deciding to keep my chain on and discard my watch.

"Take your t-shirt off, beautiful," I murmured, slipping my belt from its constraint.

She reached for the end of her t-shirt and pulled it over her head, leaving her curly hair messy. When she opened her eyes, I was already completely naked—hard as fuck and throbbing for her.

Nova's pretty eyes fell to my dick, and the tip of her tongue traced along the inside of her cheek.

Did she know she could have me whenever she wanted?

I gripped her waist, dragging her ass closer to the edge and her knees fell to her chest.

Fuck.

I was fighting for my life.

Such a perfect view.

I looked down at her, grabbing the base of my dick and I slapped her pussy with the tip. Running my dick through her slit, I spread her arousal around and watched her glistening pussy. The longer I looked at her—the more I wanted to taste her.

I started lowering myself, unable to resist.

"Miro, no," she gasped out, the suffering clear on her face. "Please. No foreplay. Just—just fuck me. That's all."

I forced myself back up, and it was probably one of the hardest things I had to do. Not having her on my tongue? That didn't feel right and with all the strength in the world, I swallowed away the urge to fuck her with my mouth instead.

She could have whatever she wanted and I meant that shit.

I breathed in, licking my lips when she spread herself wider for me.

She wants this. Probably the same way that I do.

"Fuck," she groaned, feeling my dick nudge through her slit and stroke her clit.

She was utterly soaked.

I was impossibly hard.

I held my dick, dipping the tip into her wet hole and pulling out again. The both of us let out a small moan. I wanted more. I needed more. But I didn't want to hurt her.

No foreplay?

I took my time with her, hearing her muffled moans when I started easing into her again. I gasped out at the feel of her pussy just barely around me. We weren't halfway yet, but the amount of pleasure that came from it felt unreal.

She was everything I remembered. Warm. So fucking warm. And wet. Nova's hands curled into fists on the sheets. I grit my teeth, forcing myself not to thrust into her full force.

"Take your fucking time, Miro. I have all day, right?" she spat, her eyes hard and her arms eagle spread.

I reached over her, clasping onto the front of her throat and giving her a rough squeeze. It wasn't enough to choke her. It was enough to warn her about that little fucking attitude she was giving me.

I glared down at her, and her eyes briefly widened. Keeping my dick at her pussy, I looked at her in the face when I fully slammed into her.

She gasped, but it was short lived.

I had already pulled out of her, and I was quick to thrust back in until I had nothing more to give. I did it over and over again, giving her exactly what she fucking wanted.

Waves of pleasure rushed through me—nearly flooring me. How could it feel like that? How could I be the cause of the sheer satisfaction on her face?

I'm going to have a damn heart attack.

I clenched my eyes shut, lost in the feeling of being inside of her.

There was nothing that could compare to it.

"Fuck—fuck—" she grunted, holding her lower stomach and I smirked at the sudden loss of attitude on her face. Not that bold when I fucked her the way she wished to?

"When are you going to learn to stop rushing me, huh?" I murmured, breathless and hopeless against my own self. I slapped her ass hard, leaving my hand print forming on her skin and her startled moan echoed through her room.

I fucked her and held her legs, bottoming out as her pussy tightened around me. She couldn't control her noises. Not that I wanted her to. I moaned out loud, throwing my head back as I continued to thrust in and out of her.

"Fuck," she grunted, lifting her head as she started watching me fuck her. "I—"

"What?" I chuckled breathless, denting my fingers into her skin as I held her. "You got nothing?"

All I wanted to do was make her feel good.

Watching her underneath me was indescribable, and I witnessed the very moment she gave up on glaring at me.

Her face morphed into a look of pleasure. Low-eyes, a dazed face and parted lips. Her fists uncurled from the sheets, now laying slack across the mattress as her body hitched with the force of my thrusts.

I hooked her legs around my waist, and the angle had me pushing deeper.

I groaned, grunting through a clenched jaw as her pussy enveloped me. I could have fucked her for the rest of the night and possibly the next morning too.

Nova's moan was loud, coming straight from her chest as she rode out her orgasm. "Miro—fuck."

Louder, baby.

"You feel so good, hermosa," I breathed, moaning through my words.

Her arousal dripped down her thighs, and I caught it with the tip of my finger to taste her. My eyes rolled back, but I didn't stop moving my hips and chasing every single noise she was capable of making. But my balls started tightening and I slowed down, disappointed in myself.

I'm cumming already? What the fuck was wrong with me?

I willed the feeling away, gritting my molars. It was useless. At the same time her pussy clenched, I slipped out of her and let my cum decorate her stomach.

Nova's eyes opened, languid and in a daze.

She was spent.

"Fuck," she whispered, staring up at the ceiling as her body shook. I smirked down at her, heading over to grab the tissues on her bedside table. I wiped her quickly and disposed of the tissues immediately. Returning, I found Nova lying down on her side—curled up by the edge of the bed.

I kneeled down next to her, stroking the hair from her sweaty forehead. "Oh, amor. You didn't think we were done, did you?"

When her eyes widened, I couldn't help but smirk.

There was no way I could be done with her already.

Chapter 15

I wanted more of her. I wanted more than what she thought she was capable of giving me. What part of her made her think I was only going to give her one orgasm?

Standing up, I towered over the pretty girl sprawled over her bed.

I was bare chested, covered in nothing but a pair of boxers that didn't hide how hard I still was. It hung low, catching the attention of Nova's lust-filled eyes. Her body was still shivering, feeling her orgasm roll through her even long after I stopped fucking her.

Can she take more?

I gazed down at her, smirking as her stomach tensed while her legs tightened together. She still felt it. She still felt me inside of her and if I touched her, I was sure I'd find out how wet I made her.

I glanced over her body, breathing in as I thought about the honour of seeing her like that—all naked and beautiful.

"Miro," she whispered, her voice almost unrecognisable.

I leaned down, finding her low and eager eyes when I whispered, "Can you kiss me, baby?"

Her hand planted on the back of my head, pulling me in for a kiss she didn't wait to give me. Her lips were soft—but our kiss was anything but soft and slow and patient.

It was rough, and deep enough for her tongue to touch mine. I quickly succumbed to the feeling, letting out a small groan when her teeth drag over my lower lip.

Nova was a good kisser. I could kiss her for as long as she liked—whenever she liked.

Her hand weaved through my hair, bringing me closer and I felt a shiver crawl over my spine. Her tongue rolled with mine and a moan came from her chest, finding her lips on mine to be the most intimate feeling.

I liked it, way too much to make sense.

I was never a kisser. With Nova, I found that sometimes it was all I wanted to do.

I wanted to kiss every part of her, and my mouth watered the more I thought about her thighs over my head. She quickly became fidgety, moving and groaning underneath me.

"Miro," she whimpered, and the sound of her hands moving along the sheets was all I heard.

I hovered over her, palming the mattress on either side of her head. Fuck, I wanted her in my mouth. The more she kissed me, the more desperate I became to tongue-fuck her until she came. I squeezed my eyes shut, needing it more than I could say.

"Miro," she grunted, squirming underneath me when her hand started lowering to her pussy.

I stopped, pulling back to look at her. She wants to touch herself. I glared down at her, and her hand slowly treated back to where it came from. Good girl. Did she think she could pleasure herself when I was there to do it for her? Did she know that I was hers to use?

The look on her face was beautiful.

Her cheeks were flushed, but her yearning eyes met mine and I felt myself submit to it.

"What?" I whispered, grasping her cheeks and making her look at me. "I'm not enough anymore, hermosa?"

"Wait— I'm—" I let go of her, standing up and leaving no room for a response. For the second time that evening, I gripped her waist and pulled her ass to the edge of the bed.

She gasped, letting me move her with no restraint. I held her hand and made her sit up, getting no protests from her.

I wanted her to watch me. I wanted her eyes on me as my tongue did all the work. With her knees hanging over the edge, I got down on my own and spread her wider.

She was open and exposed and I fucking loved it.

"Miro. Fuck," she gasped out. "What are you doing to me?"

Everything that I had been dreaming about doing for weeks.

I delved forward, sliding my tongue into her and her loud moan was a pleasure to hear. I groaned, running my tongue over her hole and back into my mouth to swallow. Tasting her, I completely lost myself.

I gripped her ankles, planting her feet on the mattress and she leaned back on her palms. She was spread open, showing me every part of her and it had my dick unbearably hard—torturously fucking hard.

I groaned, flicking my tongue over and down her clit. I didn't let up. One taste, and I was hooked all over again. I was hungry for her. I covered her pussy with my mouth, tracing her hole with my tongue before slipping inside of her.

My eyes rolled back, incapable of holding back on how much I enjoyed her.

Nova was gone. Her eyes were glazed over, watching me with heavy breathing and a sultry fucking look on her face. I held the sides of her ass, loving how full she felt in my hands and I squeezed her hard. I was obsessed with the way her body reacted to me. No, I was just obsessed with everything about her.

I didn't care. I didn't care that it was too soon to be jealous. I wanted to send Nova into a place only I could pull her out of, and it seemed as if she wanted the exact same thing too.

A hearty moan fell from her lips and I thrust my tongue into her, flicking in and out and hearing her startled groan.

I needed to make her feel as if she was on top of the world.

I needed her to have a seat.

"You make me feel so good, Miro," she breathed, staring down at me with her long hair draped over her tits.

I smirked against her, giving her one last kiss on her soaked hole. Standing up, I was quick to lie down on my back. My head hit the pillow and I sighed, ready to have Nova fuck my tongue until she couldn't anymore.

"Come here," I said, gesturing her over with two fingers.

Nova's face spoke a thousand words. She knew what I wanted. She was hesitant. I gave her a look that said it wasn't the time to be fucking with me. She crawled up my body, quickly understanding the message.

"Sit down," I demanded, my impatience getting the best of me.

It was impossible to wait. Nova did as I asked, straddling my face in the direction of the headboard. It was a sight that had me wishing I had done it sooner. She was beautiful from below. Her tits—her soft eyes and her long hair.

I held her waist, urging her on because her pussy was right there and I felt like a crazed man in dire need to taste her again. It was far from just a craving. It was more than just having her pussy on my tongue. I was giving myself to her, and the expression on her face told me that she knew that.

"Miro," she muttered slowly, eyeing me with worry. "Are you sure? What if I—"

Suffocate me? Please do.

I gripped her thighs, forcing her down until her pussy connected with my lips. "Sit the fuck down, Nova."

She groaned, holding onto the headboard as she lowered herself. I smirked against her. She listened. She wanted it too. Using two fingers, I spread her open and latched onto her clit.

She sucked in a breath, slightly taken aback but I felt her relax. Her hand held my hair, keeping her eyes on me as I moved my jaw and took her.

My other hand slapped her ass, and I wish I could have seen how it shook. She had a perfect ass. Soft, round and full and adorned with the marks of growth. She was a woman I had no problem giving in to, and I slapped her again just to soothe the burn with my palm.

Nova's head fell back, showing her taut neck and her heavy chest. The necklace around her neck was gold, and it looked beautiful on her skin.

That reminds me.

I was yet to give her back the earring she lost at my place.

Did I need to? Yes. Did I want to? No, I wanted to use it as an excuse to see her again. She'll kill me if I don't give it back.

"You're so fucking good at that," she whispered, but she stared at the ceiling and started moving her hips.

I like that. She's taking what's already hers.

"Yes, hermosa," I breathed, happy that she had found her comfort. "Take it and let me taste you. Let me make you feel good." My voice was muffled against her, but Nova understood and started rolling her hips.

I kept my tongue out for her, feeling it slide in and out her as she started fucking my face. I closed my eyes, imagining everything I couldn't already see. Her ass. The dimples at the bottom of her spine. Her thick thighs. I moaned with her, and I felt pleasure rush through me.

My dick throbbed as if she were fucking me—as if I were inside of her. I moaned, tonguing her all the way from her clit to her hole and dipping inside for a moment.

"Miro," she whimpered, clutching onto her headboard. "I can't—"

"You sure about that?" I murmured, sliding my thumb over her clit when I sucked her hole. It must have felt different for her. She let out a blissful moan, the loudest I ever heard and I couldn't help but relish in it.

Her reactions weren't quiet. Nova wasn't afraid of making her noises, and her little grunts and whimpers sent a spark straight through me.

I went as deep as I could go, feeling my nose push against her. I was wet all over, covered in her arousal and I licked up every bit I could.

I almost reached down and touched myself, seeking relief. I decided against it. Being hard and suffering while she was wet and pleasured made it...fun.

I swallowed, groaning out as I held her ass with both hands. I pushed deeper, letting my tongue grind against that spot that had her shaking on top of me.

"Miro," she breathed, starry-eyed as she stared down at me. "You're so—fuck. You make me feel so good."

I know.

I hummed against her, massaging her ass in the palms of my hands. When she started tensing, I knew she was about to cum. She felt like my favourite meal, and I hoped that she did too.

Nova groaned out, sliding her hands over her stomach as her orgasm shuddered through her. She came on my tongue and I let her, swallowing every drop she had to offer. I grunted, feeling irreparably addicted to making her feel good—so much that I felt my own orgasm starting to reel in.

What the fuck?

I clenched my jaw, in complete disbelief with myself. There was no fucking way.

I moaned out with her, holding her steady as her orgasm racked through her so hard she stopped breathing—stopped making sounds.

"Breathe, baby," I murmured against her clit.

She gasped out, her body losing all tension when she slumped against her headboard. Her stomach tensed and relax, a repetitive motion that showed she was still trying to get over her climax.

I kissed her pussy softly, amazed and absolutely in awe with her. My smile dropped and I frowned, forcing myself not cum. She wasn't even touching me. How could I cum? I groaned, dropping my head back against her pillow as I felt my fists tightened at my sides.

Can I fucking stop?

"Stop, stop, stop," I breathed out, squeezing my eyes shut. What was happening to me?

"Miro," Nova whispered, giving me a small slap on my cheek. "What's wrong?"

"Nothing, amor," I muttered through gritted teeth, not even looking at her.

Why is it not going away?

Nova crawled off me, kneeling down next to me on the bed and when her fingers touched my cheek, I opened my eyes to gaze at her.

"Are you cumming, Miro?" she asked softly, her eyes locked on mine. She was still exhausted—still breathing heavy. But her face was serious, and I fell into her gaze when I felt my brows furrowed.

"Yes."

She gripped my cheek in one hand, forcing me to look at her and I was about ready to burst underneath her touch. "Why the fuck wouldn't you say something?"

She was glaring, and I was nothing but apologetic.

"I'm sorry," I whimpered, feeling her hand slip underneath my boxes but she wasn't touching me.

I felt her shift, and a warm and wet mouth closed around my dick. She had barely touched me. Her mouth felt like fucking heaven, and I came as soon as she took me into her throat.

With a deep moan that came from my chest, Nova stroked out my orgasm and swallowed all of it. I couldn't take it. The world vanished, and it was just her and her tongue running over my dick.

I was breathless, never having experienced anything like that before.

Am I fucking insane?

As soon as the feeling subsided, I pulled Nova in for a kiss.

"That was so fucking hot," she whispered, her eyes teary and her lips grinning.

"Yeah?" I murmured, sliding my hand over her hair and away from her face. She liked it. She liked that she made me cum with nothing but her on my tongue. I couldn't feel embarrassed when she looked at me the way she did.

I grinned and she hugged me, relaxing on my chest with her own. I closed my eyes, wrapping my arms around her—needing the cuddle a lot more than I thought I would.

She sighed and kissed the side of my neck, hiding her face as I ran my hands over her back. "Stay the night, Miro."

I smiled, kissing her on the top of her head. "I wasn't planning on leaving, amor."

CHAPTER 16

"We appreciate your interest in our company," the pretty lady mumbled, handing me back my application. "Thank you for your time." Translation; do not bother expecting a response.

I smiled tightly, accepting the document she held out. With a brief nod, she turned on her heel and walked with ease to her office chair. I let out a silent sigh, standing up from the hard stool and heading to the exit.

That was my second interview for the day, and I was already fed up. Both had been a failure. Either I was too under experienced, or over experienced—underdressed or overdressed. Both didn't make sense to me. I just wanted a fucking job. How hard was that?

The door opened automatically and I stepped out onto the cold sidewalk, already annoyed by the heels on my feet. There were people everywhere—bustling about during lunch hour. I tucked my hand into the pocket of my coat and pulled out my phone.

There were a bunch of texts that I had missed during my hour long interview.

Jade. Spencer. Ramiro.

Spencer sent an apology. A very much unneeded one. Did he know how good he had Ramiro fucking me last night? How am I even walking? I chuckled to myself, reading his message and replying with minimum effort. He was playful and I understood him kind of.

I just didn't want to give him anymore ideas than I probably already did.

Jade wanted to know the best brand of cat food. I couldn't tell her. I'd never had a cat and quickly told her to get a dog instead. I was just kidding and her response was a disgusted face.

I smiled, walking down the sidewalk and avoiding bumping into anyone.

Ramiro's text was...interesting.

'Where are you?'

I rolled my eyes at the lack of manners from him.

Not a hello, or how are you feeling or I miss that ass so much. Just a simple text asking where I was. I texted back, frowning when he started calling me instead. Annoyingly so, I couldn't stop the stupid smile on my face.

"Nova," he said before I could greet.

Is that how he says hello?

"Ramiro," I said, watching where I walked. Everyone had a coffee cup in their hands, and the last thing I needed was someone spilling on me.

"You ignoring me?" he asked, his deep voice filled with the accent I couldn't get enough of. "What's all that noise?"

So strict.

"I'm in the street," I muttered, clutching my bag because a man was looking at me funny. "I just got out of an interview."

"How did it go, amor?" Ramiro asked, his voice gentle. I was reminded of the versatility he held. It was beyond my understanding—how he was capable of being rough and soft at the same time.

He was whatever felt right in the moment.

Nothing makes sense.

I stepped over a suspicious puddle, frowning down at my heels.

"No luck, Miro," I said, quickly crossing the road and heading over to the less dense side. Where the hell is everyone going? Interviews, too?

"Oh, I'm sorry, beautiful," he murmured, and I could just picture his familiar frown. "You know, you could always work for me."

"Yeah? In that fancy fucking dealership you hate?" I replied, chuckling when he did too. I still couldn't fathom all the businesses he had. Or the fact that he used to teach little kids their abc's.

I didn't want to allow it to make me feel as inferior as it did but I couldn't help myself.

Was he just smart or was I just too...unmotivated?

"Maybe," he said, and I heard a chair scraping in the background. "Or I could say I'd send you an allowance just for being pretty but you'll probably rip my head off, right?" I laughed, and I quickly stopped when I realised I was laughing at my phone.

Why does he have me giggling?

I stopped at the pedestrian red light, waiting with the rest of the people who had somewhere to be.

I needed to pick up a coffee and find a taxi home.

My car wasn't with me because parking was already hard to find or ridiculously expensive. Crossing the road as quickly as I could in my heels, I let out a breath when I reached the walkway again.

"An allowance for being pretty?" I repeated, grinning. "Yes, please."

"Done."

"We're kidding, Miro," I murmured, eyeing the cute café further down the sidewalk.

"You are," he said. "I'm not."

"Stop," I said, sighing. Ramiro had already done way too much. Almost two years' worth of my salary was in my account because of him, and who knows what I'd have done without him.

I just knew my mother would have straight up yelled at me that I was a crazy bitch for letting the opportunity slide but I didn't have the heart to. I grinned when he let out a dramatic sigh.

"You're difficult, aren't you?" he mumbled.

"Maybe," I said, shrugging to myself.

"Where are you?" he asked. "Do you have your car with you?"

"No, but I'll be fine—"

"Nova."

"Okay," I muttered, stepping into the warm and aromatic café. "I'm about to have a coffee in Cups & Sweets." I looked around and headed to the line.

It was a cute place—clearly owned by someone who loved baby pink and glitter. It was adorable, and smelled of the cappuccino I was craving.

"You're in town?" he murmured. "I'll be there in thirty minutes. See you soon, hermosa."

I grinned, stuffing my free hand into the pocket of my coat. "I'll see you soon."

With one last goodbye from Ramiro, I ended the call and put my phone away. He's already acting like a boyfriend. He's already acting like he's mine. I pulled my lower lip into my mouth as I looked at the menu, wondering if he knew that he had all my attention.

Do I have his?

After ordering, I took my paper cup and sat down at one of the empty tables in the corner to wait for Ramiro. Clearly I do. He was about to pick me up and I didn't even have to ask.

I let out a breath, trying to busy myself with my phone when someone pulled a chair and sat down opposite me.

Looking up, I locked eyes with my brother.

"Hi, Nova," he said, clasping his hands onto the table.

I set my cup and my phone down, already on guard and all he did was greet me. I narrowed my eyes—still mad at him. He had pulled a gun and pointed it at Ramiro with the full intention of killing him just because he was in my home. Aside from that, I couldn't forget the things he had said to me.

I didn't want to face him.

Turning, I glanced through the window I sat next to and watched the busy street. Dramatic? I couldn't care less.

"Really?" he whispered, rolling his eyes. "I come in peace."

"Oh. A few days ago would've been a good time to come in peace, isn't it?" I asked, scowling at him. He sighed, raising his hands to indicate the peace he was talking about.

I waited for him to say anything. For the first time in my life, I didn't know how to talk to my own brother.

"I'm sorry, okay?" he said, moving his hands. "I got ahead of myself. I didn't mean to scare you. As your brother it's kind of my duty to keep you safe. Don't you think?"

"Keep me safe?" I muttered, sitting up. "By barging into my house and demanding that my guest leave? You couldn't pull me aside and explain why?" I lowered my voice when I realised I was starting to get loud.

I slumped in my seat, taking a sip of my coffee as if it were a shot. Ethan stressed me out. The fact that I was still seeing Ramiro stressed me out too.

"Like I said," he grounded out, annoyed by me. "I got ahead of myself and I'm apologising for it. Your big ass head is too stubborn to accept it."

"Ethan," I said, pointing a finger at him. "Don't fucking start with me. We're in a nice café and you're irritating me. Can you go away?"

"Give me some of that," he said, snatching my cup and I gasped, pulling back just in time. The nerve of him.

"Go away," I muttered through gritted teeth, my eyes turning into slits as I stared at him.

"Why?" he said, looking around. "You're not expecting anybody, are you?"

I am and I wish you'd leave before he gets here.

"Look," he murmured, folding his arms on the table. "I am genuinely sorry, and I'm asking for forgiveness. I went there because I wanted to hang out with you, and seeing Ramiro made me think the both of you were plotting against me. It was hard for me to believe it was a coincidence, and I was mad at you."

"Well it is a coincidence," I said. "Are you going to tell me what happened?"

I was dying to know.

Ethan shrugged. "It doesn't matter."

"All of a sudden it doesn't matter?" I asked, raising a brow at him.

"Yes," he deadpanned, nodding his head.

"Why?"

"Because you're not seeing him anymore, are you? So it doesn't matter," he said definitely, and I almost laughed in his face. He paused, leaning back to look at me before his mouth dropped.

I hate how easy I am to read.

"Nova, what the fuck?" he blurted, earning a few looks from the patrons around us.

"Keep your voice down," I hissed out at him, nearly reaching over to smack him in his mouth.

"Nova," he said again, his face contorted into a puzzled look. "What the fuck?"

"Ethan."

"No, seriously. Am I crazy?" he asked himself, glancing around in search of an answer that wasn't there. "I thought we were over this. You're back to seeing him? Why are you so fucking stubborn, Nova?"

"Maybe because you refuse to give me a reason?" I asked, grabbing my cup when he reached for it again. "Tell me right now why you hate Ramiro." So I can decide if it's a plausible reason to stop seeing him.

Even then, it might have been harder than I thought and I scowled at myself. Ramiro had me, and I didn't know if it was going to be easy not having him.

"You know, Ramiro tried to talk to me. He wants us put our differences aside for the sake of you. What's happening here? Are you marrying the guy? Put our differences aside? I'll kill him with his own gun before that happens."

"You're admitting that he's willing to put my feelings above whatever fucking beef you guys have with each other and you're not," I snapped back, glaring at Ethan as his familiar brown eyes hardened at me.

"Of course he can say he wants to do that because he wasn't the one that got fucked over in the first place," he said sharply, holding the edge of the table with his fists.

"Tell me how, Ethan," I said, throwing my hands in the air. "Why is it such a secret?"

"Why do you think Ramiro is so fucking loaded, Nova? Because he's a hard worker? Because he went to school? No and I don't want you in that life. He's a dangerous man who associates himself with dangerous people. He's a criminal, but I'm sure you already knew that. You just don't care."

"Yes, I did know," I said, sick of him. "And I don't care if you don't give me a reason to."

"I'm not going to tell you why Ramiro is awful," he said, glaring at me. "You'll find that out on your own."

"So let that be a mistake that I learn from by myself," I said. "You come in here telling me that Ramiro is a criminal and I should stay away from him. You called him boss, didn't you? Does that mean I should stay away from you too?" I snapped, watching his cold eyes.

Ethan gave me a hard look, his jaw clenching. "I don't do that shit anymore."

"I don't give a fuck what you do," I said, my voice fed up. "But don't sit there and be a damn hypocrite."

He scoffed through his nose, shaking his head. "Have him tell you. Have him explain to you why you didn't see me for two years and when he does, I'll be waiting for your senses to come back."

With that, Ethan stood up from his chair and gave me one last nasty look.

Five years. Two years. Which one fucking was it?

I almost screamed out of frustration.

Nobody fucking speaks.

I let out a heavy sigh, watching Ethan walk to the exit.

At the same time, Ramiro's car pulled up to the front of the café and I couldn't help but roll my eyes at my sheer luck.

Chapter 17

I was over it.

I watched Ramiro step out of his low sports car and eye a stunned Ethan. It was a scene I couldn't tear my eyes from, even when Ethan looked at me incredulously through the window with an expression that could only be described as this bitch.

I scoffed, annoyed as I finished my coffee and set the cup back down. I was ready to leave.

Ramiro looked as good as he always did, and I suppose it wasn't a good time to be thinking of how I'd like a rerun with him. Or two. I sighed, fed up with myself and the both of them.

I need to get home.

To my surprise, and Ethan's—Ramiro walked right past him as if he were invisible. He pushed the door of the café, leaving behind a glaring Ethan as he realised he was just ignored.

I couldn't help but chuckle even though in hindsight, there was probably nothing funny about the situation.

Ethan gave me a look, his face filled with contemplation and I glared back—daring him to fuck off. Please go away. And he did.

With a heave of his chest and a shake of his head, Ethan slipped his hands into his hoodie and walked away.

Ramiro gave me a smile as he approached me, unfazed.

He sat down in the chair Ethan had just left and took my hand, kissing my knuckles without a care in the world.

"Hey," he breathed, letting go of me. "You okay?"

I nodded, grinning at him and his nonchalant self. "Yeah, I'm okay. Wait did you even see Ethan?" Of course he did.

"Yes," he said, glancing back at the spot he just left. "I'm not interested in a fight. Did you enjoy your coffee, amor?"

"I did," I said slowly, amazed by him. "Are you going to get anything?"

It was hard to admit that guilt still gnawed on a small part of me. I didn't want to feel that way but Ethan was still my brother—the only family I bothered to speak to. Why did he have to be so stubborn? Why was it hard for us to talk?

I gazed over Ramiro, finding his lips between his teeth while he examined the large wall menu. He eventually shook his head and when those green eyes met mine, I tried to hide how hard I was thinking.

'He wasn't the one that got fucked over in the first place'

I hated that Ethan was in my head. He annoyed me. He frustrated me. But he was adamant about me not being around Ramiro and I hated that I thought about it. I liked Ramiro, almost too much and there were times that I doubted I wanted him out of my life.

What am I supposed to do?

"I'm good," he muttered, pausing as he looked at me. "What's wrong?"

"Nothing," I said quickly, frowning at him. "Why?"

"Don't lie to me, please," he said, sighing as he pulled his hand back. "Do you want space? Because I'll complain the whole way through, hermosa."

I chuckled, fiddling with a pink napkin. "You won't be happy?"

"Not at all," he murmured softly, his eyes serious when he leaned over the table with his forearms. "Is that what you want?"

I took a second, only to keep him on his toes a bit and when he opened his mouth to speak, I muttered a quick, "No."

That's the last thing I want.

Even when he might potentially be dangerous, I couldn't help but want to find that out by myself. Ethan might be right. Ethan might be wrong. Either way, I was going to enjoy Ramiro until I didn't anymore.

He grinned, leaning closer. "Yeah?"

There was a cheeky look on his face—one that I understood immediately.

"Stop," I muttered, glancing around and noticing the café was packed with women—majority of them minding their business. The young girls with their friends were looking at an oblivious Ramiro. He was truly someone who unknowingly grabbed attention around him, even when all of his was on me.

"You keep telling me to stop but not when—"

"Okay," I interjected, glaring at him when he chuckled.

"You ready to go, amor?" he asked, his eyes glinting and stress-free. I wish I felt the same.

I stood up and he did too, politely taking my coat from me. With a hand, he gestured that I walk in front of him and at the door, he reached above me and pushed it open for me.

Gentleman.

I gave him a thankful smile, striding to his car and as if he were my chauffeur, Ramiro opened the door for me and gave me a haste kiss on my temple. I let out a breath, watching him round the hood until he was seated next to me.

His car smelled like him and I breathed in, relishing in the familiar scent. I sunk into the leather seat, enjoying the warmth that surrounded me. Yawning, I covered my mouth with my hand and felt my eyes water. Ramiro had completely worn me out that night. He was relentless and a very...hungry man.

I couldn't complain about it even if I wanted to.

All it did was bring a smile to my face.

Suddenly feeling tired, I rested my head back and turned to watch Ramiro drive. It was peaceful, and everything I needed—until I realised that we were heading in the opposite direction of my home.

I couldn't stop the smile on my lips, or the heat on my cheeks. He's just taking me wherever he wants.

Ramiro glanced at me, and his own smile spread across that striking face of his. What did he do to me? I was addicted to him—my own personal little drug that I had no problem indulging in.

"Where are we going?" I asked, narrowing my eyes at the side of his head. Truthfully, I didn't care where we were off to.

"My place," he said. "Or if you prefer, I can book a hotel room for us. I just want to spend the night with you." Again. We had woken up together that morning.

It was a nice change—having company and someone to ask how I slept. He had to rush off, and I had to get ready for my interviews. I would have preferred us sleeping in on the wet, and cold morning, but the both of us had shit to do.

Although, I was not as busy as he was.

"Your place," I muttered, not caring for a hotel room. "I don't have clothes, Miro."

He smiled at the sound of his name. "You don't need clothes."

"I do need clothes," I said, my jaw dropping at him. "Just let me grab a few things."

Ramiro stopped at a red light, turning to me when his warm hand rested on my thigh. "I got you everything you need, baby. Don't worry."

"Clothes?"

"First thing on my list."

"You made a list?" I asked, grinning as he started driving again.

"Of course."

"What else did you get?" I asked, curious. Was he really as thoughtful as I thought he was?

"Toothbrush. That was the second thing. Tampons, just in case. That yellow tub of lotion you use on your face—"

"Wait," I stopped him, sitting up straight. "You got me tampons? How do you know which ones I use, Ramiro?" I eyed him, and hid my smile at the same time. Yes, he was as thoughtful as he seemed. It warmed my heart, but I tried not to awe out loud in case he hated it.

He shrugged. "I have my ways."

It must have been in my bathroom.

"Stop looking at me like that, Nova," he suddenly said, turning his hand on the wheel and rounding a corner.

"Fine," I muttered, rolling my eyes. All I did was admire him, and the slight tint on his cheeks showed that I was affecting him a lot more than I thought.

He's blushing. And I was living off it. It was nice to see him on the opposite end for a change where he could barely look at me.

"Thank you, Ramiro," I murmured, meaning it. "It means a lot that you took the time to do that," It's most likely the nicest thing anyone has ever done for me. Did Ramiro want his soul sucked out of him? Or was he just genuinely interested in having me be comfortable?

He nodded his head, giving me a gentle squeeze on my thigh. "Remember when I said I'd do anything for you?"

"Yes." I still think about it.

"I meant it," he said, his voice calm as the car came to a complete stop. "We're here, mi amor. Stay, please. Do not touch that door handle."

I nodded obediently, keeping my ass planted on his seat.

How could I, ever, stay away from this man?

Chapter 18

"How old is Camilo?" I asked Ramiro, reaching forward to grab another strawberry. I was showered, fully fed and dressed in the clothes he got for me.

It was comfortable, and I struggled to understand how he paid attention to the things I liked because it was clothes I would've gotten for myself.

At first, I eyed him. Did he have someone helping him pick out those things for me? Did he ask another woman for advice? No, Ramiro was just Ramiro and the trauma of being cheated on jumped out.

He was just...observant.

I watched his side profile as I munched on my strawberry, ironically feeling at peace for the first time since he left me that morning.

"Eighteen," he answered. "Nineteen soon."

"And he lives alone?" I asked curiously, interested in knowing about him beyond the things I already knew.

Ramiro was an open book, but he was smart about what he put on the pages and I wanted to delve deeper.

I slid my hand over his thigh, finding his hand resting on his knee. He was the one who interlaced our fingers together, holding me a bit tighter when he let out a small breath.

Affectionate.

"Yes," he said, nodding his head. "Close to his university."

"It makes sense," I murmured, enjoying his thumb stroking my skin.

I didn't ask anything else, too afraid of prying.

Ramiro lifted both of our hands, giving me a gentle kiss on my palm. Was it crazy that I missed him? I looked down at his mouth, and couldn't help but stare for a few seconds.

I wanted to know everything there was to know about him and I didn't know if it was a bad idea or not. It could be. Or it wasn't.

All I knew was that I was in his penthouse and I didn't want to leave if he wasn't going with me.

"You want to know more about me, baby?" he murmured, smiling as he saw the look on my face. "Go ahead."

"I need to learn how to control my face," I huffed out, annoyed that I wasn't as unreadable as I thought.

"No," he whispered, stroking the back of my head with his palm. "I love it."

I grinned at him, scooting a little closer and he seemed happy with the contact. "Can I ask you about your parents?"

"My parents," Ramiro murmured, letting out a breath. "I speak to them twice a year. Camilo visits once a year. They're far away and they have no idea what I'm doing with my life."

"Do you want them to?" I asked, enjoying his hand on mine.

He let out a small sound, shaking his head. "I'm good with the way things are right now. I'm sure they are too. I was a handful."

He is.

But not in that way.

"You were?" I asked, frowning at him sceptically.

"That's a conversation for another day," he muttered. "But yes, I wasn't easy and almost gave my mother a heart attack a few times."

I smiled at him, loving the sound of his voice when he spoke softly. "And here I thought you were an easy, calm teenager."

"No," he said, chuckling as he held me tighter. "I've calmed down now, I think. I loved books and sports but I also liked having my own money and that was part of the problem."

Taking a deep breath in, I looked up to find his eyes already on me—silently watching me. His gaze was soft, and I moved closer to him. It was nice to hear about his family, but I had a sinking feeling that Ramiro didn't leave his parents on good terms.

I let it go and cuddled into him. Side by side on the sofa, I was contented just being with him.

Ramiro was warm and I wanted him impossibly closer. Reaching up, I started playing with the hair at the back of his head and his response was a gentle sigh.

We were in the home he took me to the first night he met me but this time, I was there for reasons far more than sex. I questioned if he felt the same. I glanced over his face, wondering what he thought of behind those green eyes. He seemed tired.

"Was your day good?" I whispered, tracing my fingertips along his jaw.

When I held his cheek, Ramiro inched closer with a shake of his head. My face softened, finding his honesty to be the next best thing about him. He wasn't going to sit there and pretend his day was better than it was.

My eyes traced over his nose until I landed on his lips, and I stopped myself from kissing him. I don't know why. It felt right to kiss him, but Ramiro always asked.

Maybe that's the issue. Maybe he's sick of asking.

Ramiro sighed, giving me a firm squeeze on my thigh. "Please, hermosa. Do you like it when I beg for you?"

"You don't need to," I murmured quietly, leaning closer to him and I watched his eyes follow me.

I couldn't think of anything else when my lips touched his, and I felt him smile against me. He was soft, and warm and I breathed in when I deepened our kiss. Ramiro squeezed my skin, but it wasn't painful. It just showed that how badly he needed to feel me too.

"I can't get enough of your kisses," he whispered, clasping his hand underneath my ear to angle my head. "The way you kiss me. I want it all the time."

"We have all night," I said lowly, pulling away for a brief second just to see his face. "Right?"

Ramiro's lips tilted into a slight smile. "I know."

He was the one to kiss me this time and fuck, did he kiss me. It was always took my breath away. It always felt good but in that particular moment, I was completely obsessed with it.

I couldn't put my finger on it.

Was it his sounds? Or the eager hands roaming my body?

I lost myself in the kiss, enjoying the feeling of his tongue on my lower lip until I opened up for him. He moaned out loud, and I gasped when he gripped my hips and lifted me with ease. I straddled his waist, feeling how hard he was underneath me—all while his lips never left mine.

I groaned at the taste of him, and the feel of him and the way his familiar scent clung to his skin. I didn't give a fuck if we took it further, forgetting how sore I was still from that night.

If he wanted me to fuck him, I'd do it on that couch we both sat on. He leaned back and I followed through, feeling his hands slip underneath my loose shorts and give my ass a squeeze.

I closed my arms around his neck, trying to pulling him closer than what he already was.

"Fuck," he whispered, furrowing his brows. "Are you still sore?"

"No," I murmured.

He stopped and pulled back, scowling at me. "What did I say about lying to me?"

"Fine," I grunted, rolling my eyes. "I'm still sore."

"I'm sorry," he muttered, planting a soft kiss on the side of my neck. "Is there anything I can do for you, amor? Anything," he emphasised the last part and I smiled at the willingness on his face. He meant it.

"I'm good," I said, kissing him again.

"Mm," he mumbled, his lips moving against mine as he spoke. "When are you going to let me take you on a date, baby?"

"Why?" I asked, smiling at the thought of a date with him as I touched his jaw.

"I want to spoil you," he answered, his voice laced with finality.

"Right now?" I asked, chuckling.

"You want to go right now?" he questioned, pulling back to look at me again. His face was serious, and I found that he way he looked at me said he really wanted to take me on a date.

"We already ate, didn't we?" I asked, tilting my head to the side.

"Why aren't dessert dates a thing?" he murmured quietly. "Let me take you out, hermosa."

My grin widened. "Now? I don't have clothes."

"You have that pretty dress you left here. It's clean, and hanging in my closet," he whispered, smirking when he kissed the side of my mouth. He has an answer for anything.

Also, he had my dress in the wash? I had forgotten about that little number.

"Shoes?" I mumbled.

"The ones you wore to your interview are nice. Do you need to get dressed, amor? You can go just like this," he said, and I let out a small chuckle at him. The heels were black, tall and suitable for a date and I wasn't going to go casual when he had everything I needed.

He grinned, leaning forward to give me a small peck on the tip of my nose and I smiled at the sight of his dimples.

"You're lucky I keep my make-up in my bag," I muttered, and I felt him lay his hand over my hip.

"Go get ready, baby," he whispered, and I don't think I'd ever seen his eyes hold that much excitement. "I want to take you somewhere nice."

And he did.

An hour later, I was in the passenger's seat of his car as he pulled up to an indoor ocean-view restaurant that almost knocked the wind out of me.

I didn't know he means this nice.

It was dark out, but the warm lighting from the restaurant lit up its surroundings and I fell in love. It was beautiful, and the calm weather and bright stars were an addition that had my jaw dropping in awe.

I lived here almost my entire life, and a pretty place with a view like that was shockingly new. I was almost offended.

Gazing out the window, I felt Ramiro's car switch off. He unbuckled my seatbelt for me, and turned my cheek with the tips of his fingers for a kiss.

I smiled. "This is beautiful."

"You're beautiful."

"Cheesy."

"I don't care," he said, and his own smile touched mine. "Let's go, hermosa."

Besides missing a bunch of things, Ramiro didn't make me feel underdressed. Frankly, he made me feel the opposite. I didn't have my perfume, or jewellery besides my earrings. In a simple dress and heels, Ramiro made me feel as if I were the most beautiful woman he's ever seen.

He looked at me as if I was and it was truly fascinating how it worked. I never had anyone make me feel that way and I kissed him one more time as a silent thank you.

His eyes lit up, and the smile on his face shouldn't have made me feel the way it did. I pulled back and he opened his door, shutting it and walking over to open my own.

I took his hand and helped myself out of his low car, feeling my heel hit the hard gravel. Standing up, I fixed my dress and wondered if I looked good enough for the second time that evening.

I need to stop.

There was no reason for me to feel that way and I held his hand, walking side by side with him into the restaurant.

I couldn't stop thinking about how good he looked next to me.

Tall, suit-covered with his tattoos being his accessory.

Maybe I'm not that sore.

He lifted our hands, kissing my knuckles as we entered the partially empty restaurant. There were few people around, and soft music complimented the interior. My heart couldn't take it.

Ramiro was greeted by someone in a tuxedo and I felt him squeeze my hand, letting me know that despite him having a conversation in Spanish—he hadn't forgotten about me.

"No reservation?" I asked as we walked to our table.

He pulled my chair for me, shaking his head. "We don't need one."

I sat down and watched him unbutton his suit jacket, sitting down opposite me with a satisfied smile. I felt my excitement rush to surface as I glanced around, happy with what he had chosen for us. And jealous. How did he know of the place? What's wrong with me?

"You like it?" he asked.

"I do," I muttered. "It's nice. Do you know the owner?"

He chuckled, nodding his head. "Yes. Are you having food? I can get both menus if you want."

"You feed me too much," I murmured, leaning my elbow on the table.

Ramiro frowned. "That's a problem? Do you want to eat?"

He's going to make me swell up.

"Dessert is just fine," I muttered, sitting up. I need to make sure I look fine. We left in a rush. Not because Ramiro rushed me. I just hated it when people waited for me.

"I'm going to the bathroom," I said before he could ask.

"I'll come with you," he said, starting to get up and I stopped him with a shake of my head. To the ladies? Ramiro acted like a bodyguard, and I couldn't help but feel flattered that it wasn't in a possessive way—more of a I just want to make sure you're okay way.

He settled back down, sighing as he nodded. I gave him a small smile, quickly heading over to the bathroom in the far corner. It was huge and smelled of cleaning products.

The body length mirror was my favourite and I quickly discovered that I was just being paranoid about my appearance.

Feeling satisfied, I started striding back to an awaiting Ramiro.

I stopped dead in my tracks.

There was a woman—and she was sitting comfortably in the seat I had just left.

CHAPTER 19

"I'll come with you," I murmured and as soon as the words left my mouth, I realised that she probably didn't want me going to the bathroom with her.

Right? I would if she wanted.

She shook her head and I sunk back down, watching her let me know she'll be two minutes. I sighed, wondering if she knew how hard it was to leave her alone while I watched her stride off.

In her beautiful backless dress, I stopped myself from reacting to the stares that followed her.

She was a pleasure to look at, and I shouldn't have felt as possessive as I did.

I ran my tongue over my teeth, quickly averting my gaze back to the menu in my hand. I made sure Nova and I went to a restaurant that served her favourite cake — or her favourite dish if she was in the mood for it.

I skimmed over the words while I waited for her, pretending that I wasn't thinking about her not coming back. Is that normal? I doubted that it was. It had only been a few seconds.

I tapped the side of the menu with my finger and looked up just in time to find a familiar face sitting down in the seat Nova was no longer using.

Lowering the menu, I leaned back in my chair and stared at the blonde woman before me.

"You're losing your touch, Ramiro. Care if I join you for a drink?" she said, her voice shrouded by a familiar Polish accent.

Ethan said the same fucking thing.

Staring at her, it took everything I had to resist reaching for my gun and shooting her face off.

I licked my lips, internally telling myself that a murder scene isn't what I planned for Nova.

"If you don't leave before Nova sees you, I will have your mother watch me kill you." The words were true, and I stared at her fluttering eyes. I was half minded to get into my car and drive to Ethan's house to break every bone he had. He was starting to piss me off—more than he already had.

I let a lot of what he said go for the sake of Nova. Seeing Anika sitting where Nova was supposed to, I started to feel myself regret ever letting anything go.

"Wait, what?" she stammered, her faux innocent face frowning at me. "Who's Nova? I don't understand. Did I do something wrong?"

"You came sooner than I expected," I muttered, tempted to do anything but be as calm as I was. "I knew Ethan was going to hire you, but this early?"

"What do you mean? I thought you'd be happy to see me," she whispered, her voice saddening and I chuckled at her.

Anika used to be a friend. She wanted more, and I never thought of her more than just an acquaintance. She also used to work for me but looking at her, I felt nothing but rage course through me. Why the fuck can't everyone leave us alone?

Was I that bad for Nova for Ethan to go to those lengths?

I glared at her, watching her eyes widen for the faintest second. She was naïve to think I was easy, and Ethan must have thought I would have been. I was easy for one person, and she was in the bathroom while I hoped she didn't think anything bad of me when she got out.

"Ramiro, what?" she murmured, scowling. "I'm confused. I saw you here and I thought I'd come say hi. I wanted to ask you—"

"Did you hear what I said? Leave," I blurted out.

Anika's innocent expression slipped away, dropping into a glare as her face hardened at me. "Or what? I'm going to upset your girlfriend? Is she going to cry when she sees me sitting at this table with you?"

I stood up quickly, and she did too. One more word out of her mouth about Nova would have ended differently. The way she looked at me, I could tell that she knew I wasn't fucking around. I didn't care if I had to kill her in my own restaurant. I cared about Nova seeing it.

"This was all Ethan's idea. I promise. I had nothing to do with any of this," Anika murmured, breathless as she raised her hands and I stepped forward. "I'm walking away, Diaz. I'm sorry. I didn't know you were serious about her."

How easy was it for her to snitch?

I didn't say anything as I observed her back-stepping, fear and regret showing on her face. I didn't have it in me to do what I should've—and that was getting Ethan in my hands. What else was he going to do besides let me be with his sister?

I turned, seeing Nova standing a distance away with a confused look on her face.

Anika was gone, disappearing through the exit. She had followed us and while staying discreet in the shadows, I had watched her. She came into the restaurant under the false pretences of being invited and I knew the minute Nova left—she was going to try and reel me in.

How fucking stupid was that?

I sighed, frustrated and annoyed as I walked over to Nova and gestured her over into a private corner.

"Who was that?" Nova asked softly, frowning in the direction of the exit. "She looks upset."

I bit my tongue, staring down at her as I thought about telling her the truth. It didn't seem like a good idea, and I didn't want to stress her out. At the same time, I wanted her to know what her brother had just planned.

I wanted to warn her—somehow convince her to stay even when it didn't make sense.

I breathed in, feeling another wave of anger flow through me. "Anika."

"Anika?" Nova repeated, her brows pinched into a frown. "You know her?"

"Yes, I know her," I said, hating that I did.

Nova fell silent and when she glanced up at me, I saw a look in her eye I didn't recognise. "Is she an ex?"

"No," I scoffed, and I probably shouldn't have when Nova glared up at me. Feeling scared of her, I started explaining. "She's not ex. She was paid by your brother to ruin our date." I winced internally, hating the way it sounded because what part of him convinced him that it'll work?

How embarrassing was it on his behalf?

"Wait," she blurted, raising her hand as she shook her head. "You're lying."

She wasn't accusing me. She was in disbelief. Nova opened her mouth and closed it again—trying to find the words. I let out a breath, taking her hand in my own and she let me.

"How do you know?" she asked, scowling up at me. "I don't understand. Why would he do that? Is he fucking insane?"

"I don't know, amor," I whispered, hoping that Anika didn't manage to ruin our night.

She did. I can see it on Nova's face.

I ran a hand over my face, already thinking of everything Ethan was about to do. He must have forgotten that I taught him everything he knew. He knew how to manipulate—coerce and I was the one who showed him how. He just wasn't smart enough to get it right and that was the part I didn't understand.

"Are you sure, Miro?" she asked softly, her eyes conveying her disappointment.

"She admitted it herself, Nova," I said, not meaning to sound as defensive as I did. But Nova believed me, and I found myself calming down when she nodded her head.

She stared at nothing with her lip caught between her teeth, and I watched her thinking face until her eyes met mine. I knew what she was wanted, and I already had my key in my hand ready for her.

"Can you take me to him, please?" she asked, and I didn't question her intentions or her decision.

I took her hand and starting guiding her through the restaurant. Anika might have ruined our evening, but it truly showed how selfish Ethan was and Nova didn't seem happy. On our way out, I murmured a quick request to the host and he said he'll make sure it gets to the chef.

She smiled when she heard it, and the little glint in her eye was gone as soon as it came.

Maybe that'll cheer her up later.

We didn't speak on our way to Ethan's house. Nova gave directions, and that was it. I followed her instructions, and found his place in ten minutes. He moved, I thought.

Standing in front of his house, I glanced at Nova as she stared at the front door. The lights were on. His van was parked in the driveway. He was home, and I had no idea what Nova was about to do.

She gazed at me, frowning. "You coming?"

I clicked my seatbelt off and then hers. I closed the door behind me and walked around my car, finding that Nova was already stepping out.

Giving her a look, I let her know I wasn't happy that she didn't wait for me.

I just want to do everything for her.

I didn't think about how upset I was about the situation. All I thought about was the way it made her feel and the ways I could make it better.

"Sorry," she murmured, giving me a chaste kiss on my cheek and I felt myself fall a little harder for her.

She sent her gaze back to Ethan's house, and I watched the rage in her eyes intensify to the point that I felt it. Nova starting walking, and she was anything but slow.

"Nova," I called, rushing after her. Fuck, how is she so quick in heels?

"Ethan!" she yelled out, taking the steps with ease before slamming the side of her fist against his door. It swung open two seconds later, a puzzled and dishevelled Ethan coming to view in his pyjamas.

Was he fucking sleeping? He looked at Nova confused before his gaze landed on mine and hardened immediately.

"The fuck is he doing here?" he spat out, not even bothering to question why his sister looked upset.

Nova pushed him hard, entering his house and I followed her. Ethan stumbled back, his mouth ajar as he stared at her. I observed and listened when all I wanted to do was the exact opposite.

"What's wrong with you, Ethan?" Nova asked, her voice laced with venom.

"You're acting fucking crazy and you're asking what's wrong with me?" he cussed at her, and it was the moment I wished Nova didn't love her brother.

I walked forward, seeing nothing but my fist meet Ethan's face before I could stop it. He fell back, eyes wide and filled with anger. Nova gasped, but made no move to help him and I shook my hand. It was tricky, and I thought she'd be mad at me.

No, she continued to glare at him and I felt relief flow through me.

Okay, that's good.

"Watch how you talk to her," I muttered, stepping back again.

Ethan was pissed, undeniably so. He stood up quickly and as if he were about to lose it, his hands curled at his sides as he stared at me.

"I will kill you, Diaz," he said lowly, and I almost believed him. Almost.

Shrugging, I let out a breath. "I didn't hit you that hard."

"Ethan," Nova said, catching his attention with a pull of his arm. "Why would you send—what's her name?" She looked over at me, scowling.

"Anika."

At the sound of her name, it was satisfying to see the blood drain from Ethan's face. His mouth dropped for the second time, and I saw the realisation hit him harder than I did.

It confirmed what I already knew, and Nova's shoulders dropped as if she was expecting him to deny it. He didn't. Instead, his shoulders hunched over defensively—eyeing his sister as if she were suddenly an enemy.

"Why would you pay Anika to ruin my date with Ramiro?" she asked, throwing her hands in the air. "I don't fucking get it. Are you bored? Is that it?"

Ethan glared at her, his jaw ticking. "What else am I supposed to do when you don't listen to me? And it obviously didn't fucking work so I don't get why you're this upset, Nova."

"Of course it didn't work," she snapped, her eyes blazing. "We're trying. What don't you understand, Ethan? Stop interfering. That's all I'm asking."

We're trying. She knew, and it made my heart swell that she did.

"You think he cares for you?" he scoffed, chuckling breathlessly. "That's fucking amazing. Since we're all here, let's talk about it. That's what you want, right?"

"What is there to talk about at this point?" Nova asked, irritation in her tone.

Ethan smiled down at Nova. "Everything, sis. Everything."

Chapter 20

"Everything," Ethan murmured, and I wanted nothing more than to wipe that smug look off his face.

I didn't want to listen to it. It wasn't important. At least not anymore. I turned from him, no longer interested in anything he had to say as I walked to Ramiro.

He had all the opportunity—all the time in the world to explain to his heart's content and he never did. As soon as he was confronted, I could see the intention to finally speak on his face.

Now he wants to talk—after Ramiro had already clocked him in the face.

His face fell. "You're not going to listen to what I have to say?"

"No, Ethan," I muttered, disappointed in the way my brother chose to handle his shit.

Anika? Really? How was I supposed to forget about his attempted sabotage on our almost relationship? What was he actually thinking? I was pissed at the nerve of him. But I was also pissed at how sloppy he was.

Where was the denial?

He gave in quickly, and I hated how lightly he thought of it.

"Really?" he scoffed, his voice louder and riddled with frustration. "You're not mad at Diaz for doing the same shit I did!"

"Stop yelling," I shouted at him, annoyed as fuck in his spotless, clean living room that I helped him decorate. "Why would I be mad at Ramiro?"

"Because he was the one that got me locked up for two years," he said, and I never heard Ethan's voice shake before until that very moment. "Not in a county jail. Or a correction centre. Federal fucking prison, Nova. And you're asking why would you be mad at him? You have every fucking reason to hate him and you don't!"

I stopped breathing and silence blanketed over us, but Ramiro was the first one to speak.

"Ethan," Ramiro murmured, approaching Ethan as he were a wild, feral animal about to attack. "You know how hard I tried in those two years to get you out of there."

I couldn't process it. My brother was in prison, and I had no clue. My mind started reeling—a million thoughts running through my head at once.

When was that?

Was it the time he supposedly started attending a culinary school in the south of France? I held my hand to my chest, staring at my brother. There's no way. How was it possible?

"You didn't," Ethan whispered, shaking his head. "You didn't. Don't fucking lie! You didn't."

"Moreno," Ramiro said, taking a deep breath in. "Nobody laid a fucking hand on you in prison and you never questioned it?"

"It doesn't change the fact that you were the reason I was there in the first place," he snapped, his face hard and his eyes as cold as ice.

"That's what you think and it's not true," Ramiro explained, and for the first time—I sunk back from their conversation. "I did everything I could to keep you out of prison. But you were caught, Ethan. You went out and attempted a heist by yourself and you got caught. How is that my fault?"

Ethan stared at Ramiro, and I could see his blood boiling. "How's it your fault? You didn't stop Luda when he fucking told the cops my plan. We were supposed to be a team, and you let him rat me out to the police."

"I didn't let him do anything," Ramiro said, and I felt my heart racing in my chest. "He panicked. The heat was on us. We had detectives crawling all over us, Ethan. Luda thought snitching on you was the only way to make sure all four of us didn't get caught."

"And you knew," Ethan blurted out, taking his rage out on an innocent ornament that went flying across the room. "You fucking knew."

"I did," Ramiro sighed, and I saw the soft apology in his eyes. "It was too late, but I knew."

"That's exactly why I don't want you near my sister," Ethan said, his finger pointed at Ramiro. "You knew Luda's plan and you let him do it because it meant he was saving your ass too."

"I tried to warn you," Ramiro murmured, no longer on the defensive side. "I told you it wouldn't end the way you wanted it to."

"Hey, Ethan. Luda is a rat ass bitch who told the cops your plan. Maybe don't do this?" Ethan mocked, but I looked at Ramiro and found a stoic expression on his face.

Everything rushed to surface. I knew why Ethan was mad. I knew why Ramiro didn't want to tell me. I listened, but I was covered in goosebumps that stayed when Ethan stepped closer to Ramiro.

"You don't remember me calling you? You were on a mission, and you hated that I was against it. You ignored me when I called you to tell you about Luda," he said, and I swallowed away everything I wanted to ask.

"You called," Ethan chuckled, shaking his head. "It helped, didn't it?"

"Two years," Ramiro said, his voice suddenly harsh. "You were in there for two years and I'm still waiting for a fucking thank you that it wasn't twenty five."

Ramiro got Ethan out.

Ethan hated that he was there regardless.

"Thank you?" Ethan burst out in laughter. "You're right. Nobody touched me in prison because of you. You forgot that's where your authority stops. The wardens? They were having a fucking blast, Diaz. A broken arm. I have burn marks all over me and the nightmares as proof. You don't know half of the shit I'd been through."

"You don't know half of the shit I did to get you out of there," Ramiro snapped, his brows furrowed.

"Two years too late," Ethan murmured. "Luda is gone because of you. You gave him time to leave. Even when you knew he was the reason I was in there, you did nothing to him."

"Where the fuck is he?" Ramiro asked, and I realised that they must have forgotten that I was there. "Tell me, huh? Where the fuck is Luda right now?"

Ethan went quiet.

"You didn't tell me that—"

"Yeah," Ramiro interrupted. "Because you've already convinced yourself that it was my fault. You're right when you say I could've warned you—or I could've done something else to let you know the cops were onto you. You're right, Ethan. We both fucked up, and it's time you accept that."

"Did you know who Nova was?" Ethan asked, and I flickered my gaze back to Ramiro.

"No, I didn't know she's your sister," he muttered.

Ethan crossed his arms. "What did you know?"

It was Ramiro's turn to fall quiet, and I looked back at him with a pounding chest. He glanced at me, sighing and it was in that moment when I felt my heart drop.

"I knew that she worked in a bank, and that bank was going to be my next target," he explained while looking at me, and I felt my mouth drop. Wait, what?

"What?" I stammered, looking at him and hoping that he'd say he was joking.

"Was," Ramiro emphasised, seemingly scared for his life as he stepped closer. "I swear, amor. And you have to believe me, please. Our conversation that night in the casino started with me wanting to know the ins and outs of Moore's Banking. It didn't happen because I forgot. That's how unimportant it was." Wow. I had no words. I looked at Ramiro as if I didn't know him.

"When you sat next to me, you knew I'd just been fired?" I asked softly.

"No," he said. "You don't know this, but that night wasn't the first night I've seen you. You worked there. You were unhappy. I thought it'd be easy having you on my side, even when you didn't know you were."

"Ramiro, that's insane," I murmured, frowning at him. "Do you realise how insane that is? Meeting you wasn't a coincidence."

Fuck. Am I overreacting? I didn't know how to feel and that was the worst part.

"No, I didn't," he defended, his green eyes conveying how desperate he was. "I didn't know you were going to be there. I saw the opportunity and sat next to you and I'm happy I did. Nothing about any fucking bank crossed my mind the second we started talking and I promise, hermosa. I promise."

"How am I supposed to believe that's still not what you want?" I asked softly, and I knew the answer before he said anything.

"Have I asked you anything about your work, amor?" he asked me, and I swallowed away the no I already had on my tongue. He didn't. But it was also the reason why he started talking to me in that casino—because he wanted to plan a heist and I just so happen to be interesting enough that he forgot about it.

I ran my hand over my face, needing to think without the two of them looking at me. I felt bad for Ethan. His experience. How alone he was.

"Why didn't you tell me you were in prison, Ethan?" I asked him, because I'd deal with Ramiro's shit later.

His voice saddened, and I forgot how mad I was at him. "Because I didn't want you to know what a piece of shit I was. It would've killed mom. Dad wouldn't sleep. I did what I thought was better for everyone and lied."

"You know you didn't go about this the right way, right?" I asked Ethan, staring right back at him. "You could've told me all of this the minute you saw Ramiro in my apartment."

"Would it have changed anything?" he asked, and I didn't know the answer to that question. There was more I wanted to know. The way it seemed to me, Ethan and Ramiro were two people who could've done things differently. There was no one to point a finger to.

Truthfully, I was more upset that our paths crossing was accidentally on purpose and it almost hurt.

Ramiro was still looking at me, and I was dying to look at him too.

"Nova," Ethan murmured. "I'm sorry, okay? I fucked up. I shouldn't have paid Anika but if it makes you feel better, it just shows that Ramiro truly does care for you. Doesn't it?"

Even Ramiro looked shocked.

I let out a breath. "Can I have the keys to your van?"

"Nova?" Ramiro asked, frowning down at me. "I'll take you home."

"Can I?" I asked again. I just needed to be alone for a moment.

Sitting in car with Ramiro was a bad idea. I hated that he lied to me. I hated that I didn't believe him when he said he had simply forgotten about his plan. He took me home with him, and it all started because I worked in the bank he wanted to rob. No, I had a terribly hard fucking time believing him and I needed to be away from him until I did.

Ethan looked between the two of us. "Yes, you can."

"Thank you," I breathed out, grasping the keys he was handing out to me.

"Nova?" Ramiro murmured again, and I finally looked at him to find his soft, desperate eyes lingering on me.

"I'm still mad at you," I said to Ethan. "But I'm sorry about what you went through. I really am."

He nodded, wiping away the tear he didn't let fall. "We'll talk again."

With that, I started leaving. Ethan stayed, but Ramiro walked after me until I reached the van I was going to drive home.

He grabbed my arm and I glared at him, even when he was gentle and had that tender look in his eyes. I was more irritated that I didn't know anything and the one thing I knew for certain turned out to be not true. I didn't forget about everything he had done for me—how sweet and beautiful he was. I just needed to...think.

"Please don't look at me like that," he whispered, staring down at me. "Please."

"Can I go?" I asked softly, and it hurt to do so.

Reluctantly, he stepped away from me and I could tell that it was hard to do. Quickly, I got into Ethan's van and drove off without a second thought.

Ramiro had gotten into his car and followed behind me until I reached my apartment building. He also waited until I was inside the building to drive off.

Shit.

Ramiro was making sure I was safe, even when he thought I was mad at him.

Ten minutes inside my apartment felt like a lifetime without him. It was quiet, and I couldn't stand it. When a knock came from my door, I thought it was him.

Instead, a bag filled with a bunch of my favourite desserts waited for me and I leaned against the wall with a heavy feeling in my chest.

Ramiro, why am I falling so fucking hard for you that the thought of this being fake stings?

I grabbed the bag and sent him a thank you text because it felt right to do so.

Only, Ramiro didn't bother responding.

CHAPTER 21

T he next day, it was hard not to constantly think about everything.

It was a lot to take in.

Our coincidental meet up. Was it as big of a deal as it was to me? Or was I just fixated on the idea that I was still being lied to? I sighed, putting the last of my products away. I hated that I had different waves of thoughts running through my head.

I was supposed to spend the night with Ramiro, and I found myself back at my place alone with enough time to drive myself insane.

It was impossible not to scrutinize everything that was said to me and the following day, I did the one thing that helped—I cleaned. Everywhere. I listened to music and scrubbed my place, realising that it'd been a while since I did so.

By the time I was done, it was dark out and not a single response from Ramiro.

He had read it. It was clear he had. And I took a deep breath in when I checked my phone for the fiftieth time. Nothing.

For fucks sake.

After my shower, I covered myself in a gown and poured myself a hefty glass of wine. Sitting down with one of the desserts Ramiro had gotten for me, I found a comfort movie and watched as if it were my first time.

Still, he was in my damn head.

Where is he? What is he doing? Is he mad at me? Am I mad at him? I didn't know what I was feeling anymore and I hated that I didn't.

In the dark, I focused on the screen and took small sips from my red wine. It went down warm, but it wasn't as comforting as I thought it was going to be.

I was finally engrossed in my movie—until a steady knock came from my door.

I froze, my wine glass mid-air and the bright lights from the TV flickering across my living room. My first thought was Ethan. He said he wanted to talk, but I wasn't sure if I was ready for the conversation he wanted to have.

There was still a chance he wasn't happy with Ramiro, and the thought left an uneasy feeling in the pit of my stomach.

Sabotaging my date by paying a pretty woman? It was an insult to Ramiro more than it was to me.

He was lucky I wasn't vengeful.

I stood up, setting my glass down on the coffee table and while I walked, I fixed my gown tightly around me. Mentally preparing myself to see my brother, I unlocked the door and it was opened by the person on the other side.

I stepped back, frowning at the lack of patience but the look on my face melted away the second I saw who it was.

Ramiro.

Was it dramatic of me to say I was relieved? Probably. I didn't care. He was there and I missed him far too much for it to be reasonable. I didn't step towards him, but Ramiro came closer and I watched the expression on his face.

He stood there, tall and covered in casual clothes as if he didn't work today.

"Nova," he whispered, his voice soft. "Can I come in?"

I nodded, stepping back to give him space. Without straying his eyes off me, Ramiro closed the door behind him and for the first time since I've known him, I didn't know what to say.

I had nothing to say.

I'm sorry? I'm not sorry? Where the fuck were you? How ironic was it that I asked to be left alone and regretted it? Typical.

His gaze was gentle, as it always was when he looked at me. When he reached for my hands, I didn't stop him. He held me and breathed in, bringing my knuckles to his lips and I wallowed in the affection I was missing.

It looked like he missed it too.

Almost too much.

"You have no idea how hard it was to stay away from you, Nova," he whispered, kissing the top of my hands until there wasn't a spot untouched by him. "I know it was just a day but fuck, it was so hard respecting your wishes. I couldn't wait anymore. I had to come over."

"Ramiro—"

"Wait," he said, his gaze meeting mine and I felt his hands squeeze me a little tighter. "I'm sorry for not responding to your text, okay? I was mad at you, kind of. I didn't like that you didn't believe me and as fucked up as it sounds, I hated that it was easy for you to say that I should leave you alone."

I ran my tongue over my lips, fighting the urge to say anything to defend myself. The way he looked at me— I could tell that he was taking his turn to speak.

I shut my mouth, and listened to him.

"I know it looks wrong, and sounds wrong," he murmured, and I watched him stare down at me with those soft eyes. "But you have to believe me when I say that I had no bad intentions when we first met, baby. Please."

"I'm sorry that I even had the idea," he grovelled, his eyes desperate as he clung onto my hands. "It's stupid."

He lifted both our hands one more time, kissing me on the palm to convey how apologetic he was. I let him do it, even when all I wanted to do was to tell him that it wasn't needed anymore.

He didn't need to apologise. His reassurance was everything I wanted. I observed the man before me, his need to fix things loud and clear and it was more than enough. He stood tall, but he leaned over and I felt his head rest on my shoulder.

"Please tell me you're not done with me," he whispered, his voice partially muffled and I lifted my hand to the back of his head.

"Ramiro," I said his name softly, and his head was lifted to meet my gaze.

In that moment—the way his eyes sent a thousand messages— I fell for him a little harder. He didn't know that the last thing I wanted was to be done with him.

"If there's anything I can do," he murmured, and he was close enough to have my heart beating a bit harder. "Just say it, amor."

I didn't say anything. Instead, I lifted my hand to his cheek and watched him lean into my hold. When his eyes closed, I brought him down for a kiss and when his lips touched mine, I was reminded of how I really didn't want him out of my life. No, not at all.

The thought stung and I kissed him harder.

"Thank you for making sure I got home safe last night," I muttered, and his response was a nod of his head. "Thank you for the desserts. Thank you for being honest with me. Most importantly, thank you for showing up even when I chased you away. I'm not mad at you. I never was. I just needed to think."

The way his eyes lit up and glowed with newfound life, I could tell my words meant a lot to him. His brows furrowed, and I felt him grasp at my waist.

It felt good to talk to him. There was nothing said about Ethan. Or anything else that happened yesterday. It was just us, and I wouldn't have had it any other way.

"Yeah?" he whispered, leaning down. "You mean that, baby?"

"Yeah," I muttered. He grinned, and I felt my own face soften at the look of him. How could I not mean it?

"Does this mean I can stay?" he asked, his smile wide and his dimples deep.

I let go of him, rolling my eyes. "Yeah, I guess."

When he chuckled, I couldn't hide how happy I was that he was about to stay.

Chapter 22

"Have you talked to Ethan yet?"

"No."

"Do you want to?"

"Yes."

Ramiro pulled me closer to him, and I sighed into his hold. I was contented, finally relaxed—except for the gruelling voice in my head demanding that I talk to my brother. What could I say? I'm sorry you were locked up and didn't tell me? I'm sorry you're traumatised? I'm sorry I don't know how to comfort you?

I closed my eyes, annoyed that I was, essentially, choosing Ramiro over my own brother.

What's wrong with me?

"Amor," Ramiro murmured, stroking my head with the palm of his hand. "It's clearly bothering you. You'd feel better once you talk to him."

"You feel guilty, don't you?" he said, leaning back to get a good look on my face. He saw right through me, and I couldn't muster up the strength to hide anything.

I sat up, fixing my hair. "I do."

I thought about Ethan's first encounter with Ramiro in my apartment. It was a situation I didn't think twice about—kicking Ethan out and hoping Ramiro would stay. The dick could not have been that good, right?

I was almost...ashamed and I ran a hand over my face.

He made it easy, though.

Ethan walked in and waved a loaded weapon around my place, simultaneously barking out all sorts of threats. I barely knew Ramiro at the time, I still feel like I barely know him.

Ethan, I knew all my life but clearly I don't know enough.

Why was it that difficult?

Am I a terrible sister?

Fuck it. I cuddled into Ramiro and felt him hold me tighter, silently deciding that I wasn't going to dwell on it anymore. At least that's what I hoped I'd do. When my phone rang, I clenched my eyes shut and felt Ramiro reach over the sofa we sat on. He grabbed my phone, and told me with a stoic voice that it was Ethan.

"Do you want to answer?" Ramiro asked, and I nodded as if it were the last thing I wanted to do. I did, quickly sliding my thumb across the screen. Ramiro watched me, and I sighed as I put the phone to my ear.

Ethan didn't wait for me to say anything.

"I'm outside, Nova. Can I come up?" he asked, and I froze immediately.

Perfect fucking timing.

Ramiro noticed, and let go of me with a frown. I straightened up, catching my lower lip between my teeth as I contemplated it for a second. There was nothing to think about. My brother was downstairs and as much as he annoyed, and irritated me—I couldn't say no. Right?

"Yeah, come up," I muttered, and Ramiro nodded as if he agreed. He must have heard Ethan's voice.

This time, however, I was hoping it wasn't going to be another battle of the egos as I pushed myself off the couch. Out of Ramiro's hold, I was left feeling cold on the skin he wasn't touching anymore. He's not going anywhere, I thought.

Grabbing one of his hoodies, I pulled it over my head and heard a knock on the front door—that familiar, daunting knock. Ethan was unpredictable, and I hated it. I unlocked and opened for him, scowling at the tired eyes staring back at me. It quickly averted to the space behind me, zeroing in on a sitting Ramiro.

"I didn't know you had company," Ethan murmured, the distaste loud in his voice.

I scoffed, about to close the door in his face one more time. He stopped me. Slamming his palm against the wood, he gave me an apologetic look that I couldn't believe. He was always complaining. There was not a single sentence that came out of his mouth since I knew Ramiro that wasn't along of the lines of an irking complaint.

Breathing in, I tried not to let myself get riled up in a two second conversation with him.

I turned, giving Ramiro a face that silently asked him to give the two of us space. Please.

"Of course," he muttered, sitting up with no hesitation.

"Thank you," I said, watching Ramiro grab his phone and keys. I didn't mean he should actually leave.

I frowned, but Ramiro already saw the question I didn't say.

"I'm going to make a phone call downstairs, hermosa," he said, his voice gentle as his eyes met mine. I nodded, observing the way he barely acknowledged Ethan who hadn't taken his gaze off him since he stepped into my apartment.

He walked through the open door, paying no mind to a glaring Ethan. Why did I think he'd at least try to be amicable? Ethan secured the lock in place, breathing out as he frowned down at me.

"You're still seeing him?" he asked, and I felt my shoulders drop.

"Ethan. Please—" I was extremely fed up. I must have told myself that a dozen times. Each time felt like the last time. Repetitive.

He raised his hands. "I'm just asking. I get it. You love him. He loves you. It doesn't mean I need to like him."

"Love?" I asked, flabbergasted as I stared at him. I liked him, yes— a lot more than I could probably admit out loud. I also knew I had feelings for him that I couldn't explain if he asked. It was an odd position— not knowing what grounds we stood on.

Ethan rolled his eyes, grabbing a chair to plop himself down on. Clearly he's the annoyed one.

"You stress me out, you know that?" he murmured, playing with a random plush he found. "You're the only family I have left and it stresses me out. It makes me do stupid shit. Shit I would have laughed at two years ago."

I sat at the table with him, losing all defence as I listened to him in my kitchen. My brother loved me—probably to the point that he was willing to do unthinkable things to protect me.

It was...too much. He was also the only family I had left. Didn't he know his actions could have ended with him having no family, whatsoever? I pursed my lips, remembering we had no contact with my dad's side, and my mother was an only child orphaned in her teens. It was complicated, and simple at the same time.

"You do stupid shit, even when you say you're going to stop doing said stupid shit," I mumbled, half under my breath and half directed at him.

"I know," he said, running a stressed hand through his curls. "I hired Anika as a test. A stupid one, I know. She and Ramiro has history, and I thought her familiarity would make him forget about you. I'm genuinely sorry."

I continued listening, watching my brother bounce his knee and fidget with the soft toy in his hands.

"Our conversation last night—I spent the last few years hating Ramiro for letting Luda rat me out. I didn't understand it. Or, I just didn't want to," he went on, his eyes casted downwards. "I believed he did it. Don't tell him I'm saying this, but I think I was wrong, Nova. Fuck."

His hand dragged over his face, exasperated and laced with exhaustion.

"Think?"

Ethan gave me a look. "Don't start. It's taking a lot to admit it out loud."

"Ethan," I murmured, my voice softening. "You're saying all this to the wrong person."

He paused. "Forget it."

I shrugged, knowing there was no point in arguing with him. "Fine."

We fell into silence, and I took a deep breath through my nose when it showed that there was a lot more that Ethan wanted to say.

I just wanted all the drama to be over. It tired me out—constantly wondering if Ethan was going to switch up on me any time soon.

"About the prison," Ethan started, his voice growing cold as his face hardened. "It's not something I'd like to talk about. If that's okay."

"That's perfectly fine," I mumbled, feeling the pity for my brother growing in my chest. "Just—just stick to your promise, okay?"

"What promise?"

"Ethan," I groaned, frowning. "For fucks sake."

He chuckled lightly. "I will, Nova. I promise I won't try to kill Ramiro again."

"That was you trying?" I joked, but I was half serious. I laughed, but it was far from funny at the time. It was quite...concerning. Truthfully, I didn't know how Ramiro didn't grab his things and run out of my life the second he saw who my brother was.

It made me think. It also made me wonder if he was still trying to prove a point. I need to stop.

"I need to go," Ethan said, grabbing his keys and letting go of the toy he had been holding. "I have a hot date to get to."

"Your life is busy," I commented, eyeing him.

He lifted his shoulder into a small shrug. "Anything to keep my mind off things."

I nodded, finding his honesty a breath of fresh air. We didn't talk much, but it helped in lessening the immense amount of guilt gnawing at me. He was fine. I was fine. Everyone was fine. I hope.

We bid our goodbyes, and Ramiro walked in a minute later. He grinned when he saw me, striding to me with open arms. When he hugged me, he kissed the top of my head and whispered something I didn't hear.

"Feel better?" he asked, his voice soft and accented and deep and everything that sounded right.

"Yeah," I breathed, leaning my head against his chest.

"Good," he deadpanned. "Hungry?"

"Starving."

"Okay," he muttered, letting go of me but not before laying a gentle kiss on my forehead. "Sit down, hermosa. I'll make something to eat."

I smiled, happy with the way it felt to be stress-free.

<h1 style="text-align:center">CHAPTER 23</h1>

"You always make the best meals," she murmured gently, setting her knife and fork down over her empty plate.

She had finished her food quickly, ending off a thankful smile and a satisfied sigh. She loved it. The dish was a simple stir-fry made with ingredients she already had in her fridge. Nova always ate as if it were the best thing she'd ever tasted and it was the best part of cooking for her.

I'd cook for her every night if she let me.

She's probably sick of me staring at her.

I glanced away—just for a second, but I was quick to lay my gaze on her again. It was hard not to look at her and each time I did, I remembered how close I got to fucking everything up. Again.

She had me stressed beyond measure and I was sure she didn't know that I was plagued with thoughts of her. I could barely think straight, let alone be logical.

Don't show Nova that there were things I'd do for her that didn't seem reasonable. After all that Ethan had done, I couldn't help but think that doing certain things were valid in a certain sense. Ethan went low, and it was hard not to go lower. You're a hypocrite. Fuck. Was I?

Nova wouldn't forgive me.

But fuck, it was one of the most difficult things I'd ever have to do.

"You still a little upset, are you?" Nova asked, frowning at me from across the table.

My eyes met hers, finding that I'd been lost in thought while she sat there and watched me. I quickly snapped out of it, setting my knife and fork down over my empty plate too.

"Why would I be mad, amor?" I asked, genuinely curious. There was nothing to be mad about. I was in her home, and she looked a bit happier than before. I had no complaints, except that I probably didn't hit Ethan hard enough.

Nova shrugged, her pretty brown eyes fixated on my own. "I don't know."

I kept quiet, following her movements as she stood up from her chair. I leaned back, knowing her intentions and loving the outcome when she lifted one leg over me—straddling my waist.

I sighed, feeling her sink onto me while her stomach touched mine. I'd do anything to keep having her that close to me.

"You don't know?" I asked softly, scowling up at her.

Did she think I was mad at her? I was—the smallest amount. I got over it the second she opened her door for me. I stopped thinking about it when I saw on her readable face that she had missed me, or thought about me once or twice and wondered if I'd show up or not.

I'm completely fucked.

"You said you hated that I asked to be left alone," she murmured, sliding her soft palm over my cheek.

I could hardly form a proper sentence with the way she felt on top of me. It's hard concentrating when I can feel her warmth. I held her waist, feeling her cotton t-shirt scrunching underneath my hands.

I shook my head. "No, hermosa. I'm fine."

I was more than fine.

"You sure?" she asked, her voice sultry when she her lips touched the side of my neck.

She breathed in, letting out a small sound. I closed my eyes for a moment, cherishing the softness of her skin and the smell of her around me. Nova always smelled good—a scent I'd recognise amongst a thousand others.

My closed eyes squeezed shut, urging myself to not get hard underneath and hoping she didn't feel it.

"Yes," I muttered, glancing up at her and the way she stared down at me.

Her hair was loose, falling over her chest and shoulders in tight curls that smelled of the shampoo she used. I had given up on hiding how easy I always was for her.

I swallowed, feeling the tips of her fingers graze over my jaw.

Her arms were lifted and closed around my neck, bringing me a little closer to her. I dropped my forehead against her chest, wondering if her heart beat was as hard as mine. It can't be.

With her hand in my hair, Nova pulled me back and I was forced to look at her even if it felt as if I were about to lose myself underneath her.

She sighed, gazing down at me with a look I had seen a million times—a look that was far from unfamiliar. Nova wanted me, and she wanted me right on that chair. I breathed in, and she did too—curling her hand around the back of my neck.

"You promise?" she asked, a slight frown between her brows.

I look as desperate as I feel.

"Yes, I promise," I whispered, concerned that she still thought I was mad.

Did I look mad? No, I didn't think so.

Nova nodded, watching her flat hand slide over my chest until it turned and glided over my covered stomach. I was practically heaving underneath her, uncontrollably so. Her touch left me wanting more, and I felt the need for her convey through my fingertips denting into her skin.

"Nova," I muttered, feeling her hand graze the hem of my pants.

I thought she'd stop there. And she didn't. With her eyes on mine, her hand fell between us and dipped into my pants.

Her lips parted, and I felt my eyes widen when her fist closed around my dick. It was unexpected—how unbelievably good it felt. She smirked slightly, realising how hard she got me. I couldn't feel ashamed. She must have known by now that one look from her had me feeling all the things that felt good.

I leaned back into the chair, welcoming her and whatever she wanted to do. If she wanted to have me, I'd let her.

No words were spoken when her hand around me pulled me from the constraints of my pants, exposing me to her gaze.

"Amor," I breathed, utterly consumed by her and her lust-filled eyes drinking me in.

"Don't say anything, Miro," she whispered, reaching underneath her to slip her underwear to the side. I almost said take it easy. I almost said wait let me taste you first. Clamping my mouth shut, I felt my jaw clench when the tip of me ran through her already wet slit.

She wants it right here?

I couldn't resist.

I groaned, feeling my eyes roll back at the warmth radiating off her. Nova had me—in ways that she didn't know. I slumped into the chair, relaxing and letting her take the reins.

She was still straddling me, but her feet were planted onto the ground. Lifting herself, Nova held the base of my dick and with no hesitation, sunk down onto me. Her pussy engulfed me, sending waves and waves of pleasure through my veins and I gasped at the same time she did.

"Fuck," she grunted, sliding her fingers through my hair to pull me into kiss. "I needed this, Miro."

"Me too, baby," I breathed, shutting my eyes when I slid deeper inside of her.

Shit. I'm not supposed to speak.

I couldn't help it.

Words could barely bring justice to the way it felt. How long had it been? It felt like forever.

I slipped underneath her t-shirt, finding the bare skin on her waist. She was soft. She was smooth. She felt like heaven in the palm of my hands, and I held her tighter when she finally had all of me inside of her. I moaned, my head falling back. Nova's lips were on the side of my neck, kissing me and spoiling me.

I didn't move her. Or rush her. She kept me inside of her, and stayed that way while her lips decorated my skin with open mouth kisses.

Yes, I needed this.

More than she could have ever known.

My hands glided over her ass, feeling a combination of material and flesh and it was a sensation I didn't know I liked. Her t-shirt was the only thing covering her, except for her underwear. I looked down, observing how deep I was and when her hands touched my shoulders, I locked eyes with her.

"Wait—" I gasped out, but Nova had already slipped me out of her. She was quick to slide down, forcing moans out of my chest and I was completely overwhelmed by the amount of pleasure soaring through me.

I couldn't get over it. I could barely believe it.

She took my breath away, holding herself steady and gazing down at me with each stroke.

I gulped, giving her a harsh squeeze on her ass. I was gifted another moan from her lips, but her pussy tightened around me and her moan matched mine.

I dropped my head against her shoulders, helping her fuck me with my hands on her waist. I lifted her, slamming her back down and with no space to breathe, I did it over and over again.

It was spontaneous. No foreplay. No teasing. Just her—making me hers with each lift of her hips and every kiss on my lips.

She gasped out, rolling her waist and I hit a spot inside of her that had her body tensing. I took advantage of it. She might have been fucking me, but I still needed her to feel the best she's ever felt.

Nova deserved nothing less than.

"Miro," she grunted, and her hands on my shoulders stiffened into a tight hold.

It was insane—fucking her with nothing but pure lust and care. She was wet, and I was hard and completely covered by her. My heart was erratic, but hers wasn't any different. I dropped my forehead against her chest, focusing on nothing else except the beautiful woman on top of me.

It was a privilege I cherished, watching her with an unwavering gaze because I, simply, couldn't get enough of her.

"Miro," she said again, catching my attention. "That feels so good."

"I know," I grunted, gritting my teeth. It felt better than good. We probably had bigger shit to worry about but in that moment, it was just the two of us pushing all those worries to the side. Like her underwear.

I couldn't say I was falling for her. No, it was more than. I looked up at her pretty face and felt her pussy around me. The two sensations morphed into one. Visual pleasure, and physical pleasure. Nova didn't stop fucking me.

She fucked me until her pussy throbbed, harshly tightening around me when her orgasm came with a small gasp from her throat.

Her body tensed, and her head fell back. When she started cleaning around me, I couldn't bring myself to stop moving her. I fucked her, and she let me—moaning through it until her body slumped against mine.

Holding her ass, I thrust in and out of her. My sounds were muffled by her hair, and it was clear she was the only one capable of having me making those noises she loved.

"In me," she gasped, using the one breath she had. "Please."

"Yes, baby." I obeyed her demands within a second.

Moaning out loud, I came quicker than I thought I would. I fucked my orgasm into her and drowned out the world around us, filling her till it dripped out of the sides of her. Nova's moans were euphonious. It raced through me and led me into one of the most intense orgasms I'd ever experienced.

With one last thrust, Nova's tense body finally went slack into my hold.

I was breathless, and so was she.

Still inside of her, I gripped her chin and brought her closer for a much needed kiss.

It was my way of sealing the deal, reminding her that I cared for her even when our fucking lacked any sort of romance. Nova grinned into our kiss and honestly—sometimes, the aftermath of her satisfied smile was the best part of having her.

"You okay?" I asked, attempting to control my breathing.

"Never better," she whispered, deepening our kiss on her own accord and I groaned out loud.

Me too, amor. Me too.

Chapter 24

"Can we talk?"

I glanced up from the numbers littered across my screen, frustrated with the interruption.

Ethan.

I sat back, letting go of my pen as I eyed him. What the fuck did he want? He stood at the door of my office, and his face said he'd rather be anywhere else than there. Ethan had his hands in his pockets, rolling on the heels of his feet.

He was the last person I expected.

I expected Luda before I expected him.

I gestured to the seat opposite me, curious on what he had to say. The usual stay away from my sister? You're bad for her?

It was almost comical at that point.

Speaking of, I hadn't heard from Nova the entire day. I had left early morning, needing to catch up on work while she went around for interviews again. Why can't she just let me take care of her? I almost smiled, until I remembered who stood there waiting for a conversation.

He nodded, sitting down and keeping his hands on the arms of his chair.

"Yes?" I asked, keeping it short. Who let him in without asking? For the sake of interest, I paid no mind to the amount of anger boiling through me.

Nova loves him. Nova loves him. Why did she have to? It would have made it easier getting rid of the curly haired rat. If she wasn't going to be mad at me, what were the lengths I was willing to go?

He took a breath in, folding his hands the way I noticed he did every time he talked to Nova. I cocked a brow, reading him but all his expression showed was that he was hesitant about whatever he wanted to say.

I narrowed my eyes at him, feeling as if I'd much rather struggle with my calculations than look at his face.

"Get on with it, Ethan," I said, my voice harsher than I intended but with no complaints.

He clamped his mouth shut, cutting off the words he wanted to say. He's wasting my time.

"I wanted to come to you with a request, Diaz," he said, his voice steady and his eyes zeroed in on me. Oh? He's serious?

I breathed in, closing my eyes just for a second. "You're asking me for something?"

The damn nerve.

"No," he said, and I could tell he was controlling himself. "A request."

"For what?" I asked, already expecting that it had something to do with Nova.

He waited a bit before answering, drifting his gaze from the floor back to my face. "One last job."

"One last job meaning what?" I asked, sitting up in my seat. He's fucking insane. I glared at him, but Ethan didn't falter. Did he want to work together? Is that it? I nearly chuckled, but there was nothing funny about him trying me.

"One last job meaning I make enough to fuck off overseas and leave you and Nova alone," he said, his jaw clenched as his eyes hardened.

He wanted to leave Nova? I wanted to express how much that would hurt her, but I couldn't. If he wanted to fuck off, he could figure out a way to do that shit on his own without involving me.

"You're kidding, right?" I murmured, confused on how he thought he could approach me with a proposal like that. Work with him? After he had it out for me? It was baffling.

"I fucking wish I was," he said, shaking his head. "But I'm desperate. You know how hard it is getting a job with a criminal record?"

"I don't care," I said, scowling that he thought I would. "What's your plan, Ethan? We do this job, you rat me out and get your revenge?"

When his jaw clenched, I knew I had struck a nerve. "I'm not as low as Luda."

"Now you're admitting it was him?" I asked, tilting my head to the side. "After all these years of thinking it's me?" I shouldn't have cared enough to argue with him, but it was hard not to.

All that bullshit just for him to accept that it was Luda who snitched on him to the cops in two days? It made my bones itch from the inside out.

Ethan breathed through his nose. "I'm not here to fight."

"I can never think of you as a brother in law," he continued, his voice much calmer. "I can't stand to be in this city. I'm fucking broke, and one last job with you means you'd never get to see me again."

Brother in law? Were we there yet?

"I don't do that shit anymore," I said, shaking my head. It was tempting—almost. He'd gain, and I would too. On top of that, no more drama from him about me being with his sister? It seemed like a win-win, but it just didn't make sense.

He scowled at me, obviously in disbelief. "Since when?"

"Since you got with Nova?" he said when I didn't bother answering his question. "Really?"

"You can see yourself out," I muttered, opening my laptop to continue with my work. Ethan was ridiculous. I didn't trust him. I barely wanted to be around him.

The bruise on his eye was already starting to fade and surprisingly, he didn't seem to hold any grudges against me for it. Or at least that's what it looked like.

I could always read Ethan, but he was right when he said prison had changed him. He was already reckless before, I couldn't imagine that this wasn't the perfect way for him to execute his revenge.

"Ramiro," he said, his voice solemn as his shoulders fell. "Nova doesn't need to know. You were planning on robbing the bank she worked at, right? I can ask her for info. If I come to you with a plan, will you think about it?"

Thinking about it meant there was a chance I'd agree.

"Ethan," I said, starting to feel myself grow irritated again. "There is nothing to think about. The answer is no. You're asking me to go behind your sisters back? No, I won't."

I could, but I didn't want to—especially with her own brother. Nova would kill me. She'd kill Ethan for getting into trouble again. It wasn't worth it and I couldn't believe I was continuing to let him talk.

He stood up abruptly. The sound of chair scraping against wood was loud, and I watched him intently as he glared down at me. What does he want to do? He was angry.

"This is your only chance of getting rid of me and you're not taking it?" he asked, almost shouting while his hands balled into fists at his sides.

"It's not my only chance," I murmured, scoffing.

"It's the one you're getting right now," he argued. "I can't believe you're stupid enough to say no."

I stood up too. "You're stupid enough to walk in here asking for favours when you did nothing to fucking deserve it. You walked into Nova's apartment and pointed a gun at me, remember? You said you'd kill me, remember? What the fuck happened to that, Moreno?"

Yes, I was still bitter about it.

"That was before I knew it was Luda who ratted me you, Diaz. Get the fuck over it," he snapped, leaning his fists against my desk.

"Get over it?" I chuckled. "Find some other way to make money, Ethan."

"Wait," he breathed, raising his hands. "I'm—I'm sorry. I just—I'm desperate. I wanted to do it on my own, but the last time I tried that—" Ethan winced, his memories flooding in.

"You're not going to convince me," I murmured, meaning it.

Ethan's earnest look dropped into a cold, harsh glare. "I knew you were too fucking selfish to even think about it."

"Okay," I said. "Go, now."

"Fuck you, Diaz," he called out, turning to leave.

Instead of closing my door, he left that bitch wide open and annoyed the fuck out of me.

Fucker. I got up, clenching my jaw as I shut my door. Returning to my seat, I closed my laptop and fell back onto my chair. He got me riled up, and I shouldn't have allowed him to make me feel that way. He seemed desperate. He'd do that shit alone if it meant I didn't help him.

I breathed through my nose, contemplating my options.

Did he need my help? Probably.

Did he feel entitled to it? Yes, he did. For whatever fucking reason, he did.

Am I going to regret it? I don't know.

I tapped my pen against a book, slowly realising that the best thing I could do in that moment was ask Nova.

I might regret it. Ethan might put a bullet in my head.

All I knew was that I needed to speak to her.

CHAPTER 25

Knocking on Nova's door always felt the same—scary as fuck. I couldn't explain why. It was a feeling that rose to surface each time I showed up at her place without announcing myself.

Would she care? I knocked twice and dropped my fist, waiting for her. It was insane how nervous I continued to feel around her, even when she didn't give me a reason to be.

It took a few moments for her door to open, and it wasn't her.

"Oh!" a red headed woman shouted, her eyes wide as they landed on me. "Hi. Can I help?"

"Uh—" I trailed off, frowning.

Was I at the wrong place? My eyes flicked to the gold plated number on the door. Yes, I was definitely at the right apartment.

She looked at me expectantly, still holding the door as if I were about to barge in.

"Who is it, Jade?" a man's voice called out, and I gazed behind the short woman to find the source of noise.

What's going on? I stood there, with my gun tucked into the back of my pants, feeling as awkward as I did on the first day of school.

Why do I even have it?

"A really tall man," she said, eyeing me with scrutiny. I grinned when Nova came rushing to the door, her smile wide as she slid past her friend and gave me a haste kiss on the cheek.

She's happy to see me.

I relaxed, calming down as the fleeting feeling of her lips on my skin warmed me up. How fucked am I if I missed her after a day? She took my hand, pulling me into her home and I was hit with the scent of warm, cinnamon cookies.

"Ramiro," Nova murmured. She was dressed in a simple grey sweatpants—paired with a light pink t-shirt that was tight on her, and also showed a small portion of her lower stomach. Pretty girl.

I looked down at her, until I remembered that I was around two people I'd never seen before.

"This is Jade, my friend," Nova introduced us, her hand on her friends shoulder. "This is Dylan. Jade's boyfriend."

"Jade's boyfriend?" Dylan said, his voice holding an accent I couldn't decipher. "That's all I am, Nova?"

"Well," Nova trailed off, shrugging.

He laughed, getting up from the sofa he sat at to give my hand a brief shake. Nova's friends. I introduced myself too, trying not to come across as cold and lifeless.

I didn't know how to act around new people. It'd been an issue since school. My social abilities were limited, and it was part of the reason I fell so hard for Nova—it was easy around her. She just made it feel easy.

"Are you Nova's boyfriend?" Jade asked, her eyes glinting as she clasped her hands together. Dylan also looked curious, and his arm fell around Jade.

"Yes," I said before Nova could—and her little smile told me she approved.

Jade grinned. "I knew it. Are you the guy who took her home after—"

"Jade!" Nova gasped, cutting off her friend.

Her face faltered. "Fuck. Sorry—"

"Wait," Dylan intervened, frowning. "After what? I want to know."

"It's none of your business," Jade snapped, annoyed and I couldn't help but chuckle.

Perhaps they're not so bad.

I looked down at Nova, finding a blush tinting her cheeks. She talked about me, and I guess her friend couldn't be discreet about it. I didn't care. I liked that she involved me in her life even when I wasn't around.

"What?" Dylan asked, confused as he scowled at his girlfriend. "None of my business? You were just about to say it before Nova stopped you."

"I don't care," Jade said with finality, crossing her arms. "Stop being so damn nosy."

Dylan scoffed in confusion. "You make no sense."

"I've been dealing with this the whole day," Nova whispered, her eyes planted on the arguing couple before us. Dylan almost sounded…Korean. It was very faint, as if he had worked there for a while.

"I'm sorry," I said apologetically, and Nova offered me a small and stunning smile. For a moment, I wished we were alone. I didn't get to kiss her. Or feel her. That would have been inappropriate, right?

The urge was strong, but the urge to respect her around her friends was stronger and I kept my hands to myself—for the time being.

"Are you done fighting with me?" Jade asked, glaring at her boyfriend. The argument was playful—far from serious. I wondered how long they were together for. It seemed like years.

His jaw dropped. "I was never fighting with you."

"Clearly you were—" Jade argued, quickly being cut off by the dinging of an oven timer. Oh, that's where the smell was coming from. Nova walked over to her kitchen, grabbing oven mitts along the way.

She pulled out a baking tray lined with parchment paper, and at least twenty cookies were freshly made.

"It's hot!" she shouted in Dylan's face the second he reached for one. "My God."

Jade laughed out loud, crackling at how scared Dylan was. Nova set it down on top of the stove, discarding the oven mitts.

"We're going to be late, Dylan," Jade murmured, looking down at the gold watch on her wrist. "We should've left ten minutes ago."

"You have to give me two minutes, honey," he begged. "They're cooling down."

"Fine," she said, rolling her eyes. Nova seemed proud of her handiwork, and everyone was obviously keen on it. It did smell unbelievably good. Dylan was practically salivating, and he didn't wait.

"Can I?" he asked Nova for permission to grab one, and she nodded her head. He grabbed two—one in each hand—and it was obviously still hot because he started eating immediately. When he moaned out loud, Jade gave him a small slap on his arm.

"Behave," she told him. Nova had already started placing some in a clear container for them to take home, giving them strict instructions on not to close the lid until it's cooled down. The both of them nodded in reply.

"Okay we really have to go. Dylan's mom will kill us if we're super late," Jade murmured, giving Nova a tight and lengthy hug.

"It was nice meeting you, Ramiro," she said, grabbing her bag and belongings.

"It was nice to meet you too," I said, giving her a polite smile. Dylan walked out, waving with his cookie as he backtracked through the door.

Jade groaned, having to close the door because her boyfriend's hands were clearly occupied. When Nova and I were finally alone, I didn't wait to pull her in for a kiss and as if she were expecting it, her arms closed around me. My girl.

It was always a breath of fresh air kissing her. It released the tension in my body. It warmed my soul. It showed me that at the end of a fucked up day, I'd have her to turn to and damn, what a privilege that was.

"I missed you," she breathed.

"Baby," I murmured, sliding my hand over her back. "You have no idea how much I missed you. Come here." Her lips were soft, tasting of the familiar cherry balm she always used. I kissed her deeper, wrapping my arms around her waist and feeling her exposed skin.

There's no better feeling.

There's nothing better than just...being around her.

Nova grinned against me, standing on the tips of her toes. Even then, I had to reach down to kiss her. I pulled back from her before

I got carried away, still tasting her on my lips. Breathing in, I attempted to calm my beating heart.

One day, she's going to give me a heart attack.

With one last peck on her forehead, I paid no attention to the longing I still felt for her. She grinned, walking over to her tray of cookies and grabbing one.

"Yes, please," I said before she could ask. She laughed, showing her perfect smile and the little dimple in the corner of her mouth. So stunning. I'll never get sick of saying it.

"Brown sugar cinnamon chocolate chip," she murmured, holding it out for me to have a bite. She pulled back at the last second, frowning.

"You're not allergic to nuts, are you?" she asked. "I can't remember if we've ever had anything with nuts."

"I'm not," I said. If I was, I'd have probably felt my throat closing the second I stepped into her apartment. She smiled, immediately happy.

"Good," she said, holding my chin as she fed me. "I hope you like it."

I took my first bite, instantly knowing why Dylan was obsessed with Nova's cookies. It was amazing. I closed my eyes, savouring it. Warm, soft—fresh out of the oven. I wanted more, and Nova offered it to me in my hand instead. Finishing it, I took her hand and thanked her with a kiss on her knuckles.

"Did you like it?" she asked, her eyes hopeful.

"You made this from scratch?" I asked, scowling at her.

She scoffed. "Yes, I did."

"I don't believe you," I murmured, pulling her waist closer. "Can I have twenty, please?"

Nova's laugh was, singlehandedly, my most favourite sound she ever made. I kissed the side of her neck, breathing in the smell of her subtle perfume that was an incredible pair with the aroma still in her apartment. It was—by far—a combination I didn't expect to fall in love with.

I closed my eyes, burying my face in the crook of her neck. Her skin was warm, and soft and I couldn't help but run the tip of my nose over it.

"Boyfriend, huh?" I breathed, slightly pulling her top back to kiss her collarbones.

"You said yes before I could say no," she said, her little mischievous tone the reason for the smile on my face.

"Oh, yeah?" I murmured. "You were going to say no?"

"Maybe," she whispered.

"Why?"

"I don't think I've been asked, Miro," she said, shrugging her shoulders.

I pulled back, lifting her chin. "I'm yours, hermosa. Am I not?"

"Yes." Her answer came with no hesitation, and I couldn't help but crack a smile at the pretty girl in front of me. Her necklace sat perfectly at the bottom of her neck, and I traced the linkages with my thumb.

"Good," I said. "That means you are mine, yes?" Her response was a nod, and my smile widened at her eagerness. It was already established a few rounds ago, and Nova didn't seem to forget. I couldn't, either. It was all I thought about for days after.

"My girlfriend," I whispered, kissing her on the bottom of her throat. Her breathing was unsteady, and my lips barely touching the side of her neck allowed me to feel her racing pulse. Mine wasn't any different. If she touched my chest, she'd know that I was anything but calm.

I pulled her waist, guiding her to my lap as I sat down.

I could never get enough of her.

"How was your day?" I asked, playing with the ends of her loose curls.

"It better than I thought it'd be," she said. I lifted my hand, touching the diamond in her lobe. It was a present from me—one that I left on her pillow when I left far too early one morning. She loved it, and it was gorgeous on her. I need to spoil her more.

"Yeah?" I murmured, looking down at her thighs on me. "I'm happy you had a good day, amor."

Already thinking of my next gift to her, I came to the sinking realisation that I had never given Nova flowers. Does she like flowers? What's her favourite kind?

Was she a mixed bouquet person, or did she like a specific flower? Gazing down at her bracelet, I noticed a little flower charm, and I might have seen the same one somewhere in her place. Embroidery? I couldn't remember. I knew what it looked like. I didn't know the name.

I need to find out without asking her.

"How was your day?" she asked, staring down at me with genuine interest. "Anything surprising?"

"Kind of," I muttered, contemplating whether or not I should tell her about Ethan.

"Like what?" Nova asked curiously, tilting her head to the side.

"I had a visitor."

Epilogue

Visitor?

Ramiro had his fingertips absentmindedly running along the hem of my pants—an action he probably wasn't even aware he was doing. With his eyes on me, I pushed closer to him. I was curious, as I'd always been about anything and everything. But there was an ominous look on his face that had me worrying.

"Who?" I asked softly, frowning.

Please don't be Ethan.

Why would it be Ethan? He wanted nothing to do with Ramiro. Or it seemed that way. I sighed, sick of thinking about Ethan.

Even saying his name had me exhausted. I just wanted a peaceful night with Ramiro. When was the last time I was granted that privilege? Probably just a few nights ago. I felt him sigh, but I pursed my lips and hoped that the conversation wasn't about to steer into the direction of my brother. For the umpteenth time.

"An old friend," he said, his voice soft. "It just brought up so many memories."

I blew out a breath, relieved. "An old friend? From school?"

"No," Ramiro, his deep voice accompanied by that accent I couldn't get enough of. "Just—an old friend."

An old friend meaning what? I must have tensed unknowingly because Ramiro pulled back to look at me. No, I wasn't jealous. Far from. I didn't care about Ramiro's past. Sort of.

I frowned, irritated with myself but Ramiro's lips pulled up into a cheek grin that had me rolling my eyes.

At least it's not Ethan.

"Do not say it," I muttered, scowling at him. His hand lowered to my waist, and I felt his skin touch my own.

I was covered in a t-shirt, but he slipped underneath the fabric and I welcomed the feeling of his familiar hand. It always felt good. It always flooded my memories with our first night.

My body went warm, but Ramiro kissed my temple and I thought about how gentle he sometimes was. Or I maybe I was wrong and it was most of the time.

And the times he wasn't just made it so much sweeter.

How many times have I told myself to behave?

"Nova," he breathed, lifting my chin with the tips of his fingers.

"Who's the old friend, Ramiro?" I asked, coming off a bit stronger than I intended. All he did was smile—that beautiful, dimpled smile that had me glaring at me.

Did he enjoy it when I felt an unearthly amount of jealousy flow through me? Was that it?

I thought about Anika.

The woman Ethan had paid to distract Ramiro.

He had mentioned they were old friends—old colleagues. 'It brought back so many memories' Did Ramiro know that I'd literally kill him? He chuckled, pulling me a bit closer and I felt his lips on my skin.

"Not a woman, my love," he breathed. "Even if it was, why would I sabotage what I have right here, huh?" His lips grazed over the shell of my ear, and I supressed a shiver because I didn't want him to think I was affected by him.

But of course he knew that I was.

He made it hard to hide how I felt.

"You promise?" I murmured, hating how vulnerable I sounded.

At the same time, was there anything wrong with dropping the walls a bit? Ramiro knew how I felt. I knew how he felt. It was hard pretending that I wouldn't be covered with bitterness at the thought of him with someone else.

Ramiro shifted, pulling me on top of him instead. I was across his lap, and my arm around the back of his neck rested on the sofa. When he spoke to me, I watched for nothing but the truth and his eyes conveyed just that.

"Yes, I promise," he said, and I felt his hand on my thigh. "Mi amor, yo soy tuyo. I can't picture not having you like this. Not kissing you like this." His lips were soft against my cheek, and I felt my eyes flutter at the gentle feeling.

Before I could begin to question things, Ramiro was right there to give me a friendly reminder to stop fucking overthinking.

He squeezed my thigh and for two seconds, his touched showed on my skin when he let go of me. Was it crazy to want more? It didn't feel like I was supposed to want more from him. I already had him. He already showed me everything I wanted and needed, and perhaps that was the reason I was constantly craving him.

He breathed in, running his nose along the side of my neck. "You're perfect, Nova. My beautiful girl."

My heart was already racing, but his words pushed me over the edge. Spread across his lap, I couldn't do anything else except palm the back of his head and kiss him.

Our lips met—slow and deep. It was nothing short of breath-taking. He groaned, and the tattooed hand my thigh tensed across my flesh. It was too much. It shouldn't have made me ache the way it did. I went to push myself up, an attempt at getting away from him before I fucked him on my sofa.

He didn't let me.

"Where are you going, baby?" he whispered, bringing me right back to him.

I was engulfed by his hold, incapable of moving again. I could, but I couldn't find it in me. I liked being held by him—surrounded by him. I was on his lap, breathing in the familiar scent that clung onto him.

"Nowhere," I murmured, my gaze meeting his own.

Ramiro was hard, and despite the expressionless look on his face, his eyes couldn't hide what his body also couldn't. I sighed, running my hand over the back of his head. I didn't know his thoughts. Or his intentions.

Admiring his face, I wondered if we were on the same page.

His breathing was controlled, but purposefully so and I almost smirked when his hand on my waist held me a fraction tighter.

Was I crazy for wanting to test the waters?

"Why are you getting up?" he asked, and I felt his hand weave into my hair.

With a gentle tug, my head was pulled back. Part of me couldn't understand how Ramiro made the things he did to me feel good. It was never out of bounds. It was always what I wanted—as if Ramiro had studied me, even long before he met me.

I breathed in, enjoying him.

My neck was exposed, open to his kisses and his lips grazed over the front of my throat.

"I'm not," I murmured, closing my eyes. His mouth was warm—so soft. He kissed me harder, and I almost moaned and told him to take the both of us to the room. I didn't.

"I know," he whispered, and a hand slipped between my thighs.

He didn't venture further than that, even when I wanted him to. I ran my hand over the chain around his neck, needing his shirt gone before I took it off myself.

"You're going to take this off or should I?" he murmured, his tone gentle as if his fingers weren't running along the front of my underwear.

I was covered. But the cotton material was thin. It did nothing to ease the sensation of his fingertips tracing along my clit.

"Miro," I breathed out his name, incapable of telling him that he was the one who should take it off for me.

He smirked, moving the neckline of my t-shirt to lay a patient kiss my shoulder. My body was starting to warm up. It left my cheeks hot. It made my breathing unsteady. I looked down at Ramiro underneath me, finding his relaxed demeanour the hottest part of him.

So calm. His dick wasn't. He was undeniably hard, and I yearned to take care of that for him.

"Right here?" I asked, running a flat hand along his chest.

"Why not?" he asked, and I was immediately lifted by his hands on my waist. I gasped, feeling my back hit the sofa before I could fathom the position he was putting me in.

I was spread across the couch, lying on my back and his hands pushed my thighs apart. There was no restraint from me. He could tie me into that position if he wanted to until he was completely sated. Insane? Maybe.

"Ramiro," I murmured, feeling my chest heaving. Right here? On the couch? It wouldn't be our first time but still, the risky feeling was there to stay.

Ramiro paused on top of me, staring down with those low, needy eyes. "What's wrong?"

"Nothing. Fuck. Nothing's wrong," I whispered. I was honest. There wasn't anything wrong. Except perhaps that my pussy was throbbing and I needed him to fuck me.

"Good," he breathed, dipping his face into the crook of my neck. "Because I'm not going to fuck you, hermosa."

I let out a small noise, but his hand was on my mouth before I could voice my complaints. He's not going to? The thought was unfathomable. I started squirming underneath him, feeling desperate for a fuck I'd received countless times.

"I don't want to hear a single complaint from you, mi amor," he said, his eyes locked in with mine. "Yeah?"

I nodded, and his hand slowly left my mouth. When he grinned, I felt myself calm down. When he lowered himself, I started to feel myself grow nervous again.

Fuck. He's not going to fuck me. He's going to taste me. I groaned, lifting my hips when his hands looped over the sides of my underwear. He had that mischievous smirk on his face, watching himself pull the only thing covering me over my legs.

I swallowed hard, fighting every part of me that wanted to tell him how badly I wanted it.

"You're so patient, baby," he whispered, kissing my stomach.

Instead of venturing lower, he kissed higher until his mouth closed around my nipple. I groaned, starting to squirm again. There was only so much teasing I could take.

I gripped his hair, giving him a soft tug to make sure he looked at me. "I'm not."

He smiled as if he knew that I was anything but patient.

With his hand underneath my knee, Ramiro lifted my leg and allowed me to rest it over his shoulder. I was open. He saw every intimate part of me and with that incredibly lust-filled look on his face, I wondered if he knew how good he made me feel.

When he breathed in and closed his eyes, Ramiro's lips closed around my clit and ripples of pleasure rushed through me. My moan escaped me before I could stop it. It was loud. It resonated through my living room.

Ramiro enjoyed it, showing it with a small smile and a quick glance up at me.

"Fuck," he whispered, his mouth still latched onto my most sensitive spot. "I missed you, mi amor."

There was nothing that could compare to the feeling of a warm, wet tongue—tracing my clit and through my slit. Nothing. I propped myself up onto my elbows, needing to watch him. My thighs were over his ears, and his hands were holding me right there. It felt good. It felt better that he enjoyed it.

He moaned and I did too, losing myself and forgetting that we were in the living room. I couldn't think of anything except Ramiro making sure I was taken care of. Maybe it's taking care of him too.

I hope he doesn't think we're going to stop here.

"You taste so good," he murmured, and I was sure I saw his eyes roll back when his tongue dipped into me. I gasped, feeling him slide his tongue inside of me and flick. Fuck. He pulled out, only to dive in as deep as he could go. He tasted all of me—felt all of me.

I was floating on a fucking cloud. I ran my hand over his thick, dark hair. All I saw was his peaceful closed eyes, and all I felt was his tongue roaming my pussy as if he was attempting to memorise all of me.

He is.

"Miro," I gasped out, his tongue running from my hole all the way to my clit and when he sucked, I clenched my eyes shut. How could it feel like that? I started to feel pulses of heat rushing through me, and all I could do was lie there and take it.

"So perfect, hermosa," he breathed, pulling back just to kiss the inside of my thigh.

He found his way back to my clit. He wrapped his lips around me, and that was it. I was impatient before and in that moment, I reached my absolute limit. I grabbed his head, forcing him to look at me.

"Ramiro," I whispered, my eyes desperate. I needed him to fuck me. "Please."

"Please, what?" he asked, cocking his head to the side.

"Can we go to my room?" I asked, still breathing heavy. He saw what I needed. It was obvious. I wanted him inside of me. It was all I had in my mind.

"Yes," he said, and I started to get up until he pushed me back down. "But I'm not done here."

Fuck.